PRINCE OF DARKNESS

Megan strolled back to the guest house, drinking in the heady perfume of the roses that hung over the path, lit only by the moon that cast a silver veil over the ancient, meticulously kept garden. Somewhere in the distance, a fountain murmured.

Impulsively, she stepped onto a stone bench to pick a rose that glowed blood-red in the warmth of the night. She turned and the air grew chill as she saw the weapon shining like a scream of terror in the moonlight.

She knew in an instant that it was intended for her.

CLOUDS
OVER
VELLANTI

by
ELSIE LEE

A DELL BOOK

Published by
Dell Publishing Co., Inc.
1 Dag Hammarskjold Plaza
New York, New York 10017

Dell ® TM 681510, Dell Publishing Co., Inc.

ISBN: 0-440-11133-1

Printed in the United States of America

First Dell printing—February 1979

CHAPTER ONE

"How do you feel, Miss Royce?" the nurse asked with professional impersonality. "Another whiff," she decided, plonking the smelling salts under Megan's nose until she coughed feebly. "All right, you'll do." Mrs. Kitchell capped the bottle efficiently and thrust it into the pocket of her crisp, white uniform, surveying Megan's limp body. "Lie there," she directed. "Half an hour; go to sleep if you can."

"Really, I feel quite all right," Megan objected.

"Hah! In the words of the old joke, "Just yo' shake yo' haid." Mrs. Kitchell tucked a pillow in place and tossed a light blanket over Megan's feet. "Thirty minutes! Close your eyes."

It was undeniably peaceful in the shaded quiet of the Infirmary; there was only a faint rustle of paper, a muted telephone chime, while Megan lay with her eyes obediently closed.

"Time to think, to face up; you can't avoid it any longer . . . State the facts: you've had three shocks in six months, two emotional and one physical. I could have taken any two, but the appendectomy was the final blow. Mother's dead, Bob's walked out on me, I haven't a penny beyond my salary, and I'm apparently not strong enough to earn it.

"A pretty stupid situation, Megan Royce, for which you've no one to thank but yourself!" Bitterly, she reviewed the past year: she was twenty-six years old and still had no more judgment than a lovesick teenager . . . falling for a calculating opportunist who made every use of her stupidity. Face it: Megan was just green, too dumb to identify a cad who encouraged her to spend her small inheritance after her mother's heart attack.

"Sell the house for what it'll bring, honey," Bob had said. "There's not much worth keeping, but make a clean break anyway . . . Find a nice apartment in the right part of town; buy some modern furnishings; give yourself the right background."

It had seemed sensible to let Bob find the place, help choose fabrics and carpet, and hang pictures and gleaming kitchen pots . . . Because once he was stabilized with the ad agency, this would be their home. Why not make it right, from the start? It would be silly to invest her few thousands, to scrub along with shabby cheapness, only to have to do the job twice.

Dispassionately, Megan wondered how long Bob had meant to use her for *his* background, to provide superb buffets for his potential clients. True, he had paid for food and liquor, but it had been Megan who had planned recherché menus, marketed, cooked, served, washed up . . . exerted herself to impress, parted with a choice recipe for an important wife—and she had paid for laundering guest towels and damask napkins. It had seemed unthinkable to use even the most expensive paper goods—equally unthinkable *not* to use the treasured Canton soup tureen for Swedish meatballs, curry or lobster Newburgh.

"A major conversation piece!" Bob had chortled.

"Oh, forget it, sweetie—what could possibly happen to it? It was made to be used, after all."

So they *had* used it, and the Revolutionary silver serving spoons. And they had put the tossed green salad (or six pounds of shrimp on ice cubes) in the cut-glass punch bowl . . . and Megan had got used to saying casually, "Oh, do you like it? One of my great-greats was a whaling captain; he brought it round the Horn, about 1820. . . ."

All status—but for Bob, not Megan, and it had ended abruptly, too soon for both of them. It had been necessary to admit that he had been transferred to Los Angeles, and necessary—after her innocent inquiries—to admit to herself that he adhered to the principle of "He travels the fastest who travels alone."

"*What* wedding? Ours, I thought, but I gather I was mistaken," she had said, pinning the tattered rags of her pride in place and standing up. "Well— have a good trip," she added, "and before you go— leave your keys on the table." She had felt a faint triumph at his stupefied expression. He'd come prepared for unpleasantness, and she'd taken the wind from his sails. It had been small comfort; her own sails had been drooping, too.

She had turned away indifferently, and after a second she had heard a metallic clink, angry footsteps, and the slam of the door . . .

A month later, Megan had awakened to stabbing pain, alone in predawn darkness. "Alone. Alone." It had become a rhythmic underbeat in her mind, even while she had smiled over the Get Well cards, smiled at girls from the office tiptoeing in to visit, smiled thanks for the office-collection flowers.

"Where's your young man?" Dr. Ames had asked

gruffly, taking advantage of being her father's boyhood friend.

"Transferred to Los Angeles."

"Going west to live, eh?"

"No, it was a—mistake."

He raised his shaggy eyebrows at the involuntary throb and flagging of her pulse. "Lucky you found out in time."

"I—didn't," she said after a moment. "How soon can I go back to work, Uncle Joe?"

"Three months, maybe."

"Three *months*? But I can't . . ." Megan began to cry weakly, despairingly, while Dr. Ames' practiced fingers caught the uneven pulse flicker of fright.

"Apply yourself to getting well, young lady, and perhaps you'll confound me," he had said soothingly; but even though Mrs. Ames had cleverly bullied Megan into a postoperative visit, it had become evident after two weeks that her financial predicament was obsessing her and retarding her recovery.

"Very well," Dr. Ames had agreed, finally, "but it's a full two months too soon, and if you come apart at the seams, remember I told you so, Megan! You'll pay twice as heavily later."

Later was now, and how right he had been. Megan sighed dully. Primed (most unethically) by the surgeon, her boss, Dr. Innisperg, had decreed: "Hours, ten to four; milk and a vitamin pill each morning; a half-hour's rest after lunch; *no* filing." For two months the Department had supervised her vigilantly, and Dr. Ames had nodded cautious satisfaction at weekly checkups.

Then Dr. Innisperg had gone to a Geological Congress, Mr. Johanssen had taken a two-week ski vacation, Susie had caught a chest cold, Lyn had got snowbound in Manhasset—but there were still Shaftel, Hamilton and Zhondek, who were preparing two vital reports.

"Will you come in early and stay late, if we pay for a taxi night and morning?" they had asked, desperately—but by the time Lyn and Susie had returned, the damage had been done. Megan was back in harness, scarcely aware that her weariness was total exhaustion. While the boss was away, she had neglected manicures, shampoo, freshly pressed suit. He'd be back tomorrow . . .

Megan had dragged herself from her bed on Sunday and gone robotlike about the task of good grooming—and twelve hours later, answering the buzzer, she had suddenly felt a peculiar warmth succeeded by clammy coolness sweeping over her . . .

"How do you feel, Miss Royce?" The nurse held Megan's wrist in cool fingers, concentrating on her wrist watch.

"How did I get here?"

"Zhondek and Johanssen carted you in like a sack of flour and dumped you." Mrs. Kitchell abandoned Megan's pulse. "Can you stand up? Dr. Innisperg's waiting for you."

"He'll miss his train!"

"So?" The nurse stared over the blanket she was refolding and raised her eyebrows. "Surely you're not so *spinster* as to think a railroad train more important than you?" Megan giggled feebly. "That's better. Come along—and don't lose your perspective!"

She settled Megan in an office chair, turned on Dr. Innisperg's desk light, and eyed her thoughtfully. "You're young and intelligent. You know health

9

comes first. There's a lot of living ahead of you: don't ruin it with false pride. Beg, borrow or steal—take all you can get and ask for more—but *get well!* So long . . ."

"So long, and thanks . . ."

Megan sat in the dimly lit office, staring at the immense kunzite crystal paperweight . . . hearing the bustling tick of the desk clock that had to be wound each morning, but would never be replaced because it was the first thing Mrs. Innisperg had ever given her husband . . .

It was all very well for the nurse to be bracing, but Megan had a distinct sense that the tumbril was approaching Madame Guillotine . . . As if on cue, Dr. Innisperg burst energetically through the door from the hallway, striding forward to slide into his chair, saying, "Megan, sorry I was delayed . . . feeling better, I hope?"

"Yes, can't think what came over me," she began, but he leaned back, eyeing her expressionlessly through faded blue eyes set among myriad wrinkles acquired from squinting across deserts, ice floes, and snow-capped mountains, and her voice faltered into silence.

"Exhaustion due to disobedience," he said—and let it lie there, while he lit a cigarette.

"I'm sorry . . ."

"You understood my instructions; you accepted them. Am I not to go away for two weeks without returning to chaos?"

"The snow," she extenuated, imploringly. "Susie had a cold, the reports—and I did take taxis . . ."

"And did *not* eat properly nor rest. In two weeks you've undone all the progress of two months," he returned dryly. He raised a quelling hand as Megan opened her mouth. "Don't interrupt me, please." He pursed his lips consideringly, as though selecting words for a report on Lower Devonian sections in Ethiopia. "Your doctor told you not to return to work for three months. We tried it because you insisted, but now we know you're not to be trusted to follow orders. We also know you will now need not three, but six months to repair the damage."

Megan gasped protestingly, but Dr. Innisperg ignored her. "So you will take a leave of absence immediately," he stated mildly. "I've spent five years training you for a long-range future, and I won't have it ruined by your silliness." Crushing out his cigarette, he smiled at her. "You were my right hand here; you can be replaced—what I can't replace is your know-how when we open a branch in Paris or Rome. I've long since decided you'd set up and manage the first new office, with salary commensurate." He chuckled at her stunned face. "*Now* do you understand why you must regain your health? For six months, you're to get completely away! Sublet the apartment, go abroad, polish up your languages . . . and Madison will pay two hundred a month toward living expenses."

Megan sat silent, shocked. "You mean, if I go away for six months I can come back—otherwise I'm fired?"

"Yes . . ."

At nine o'clock, Megan still sat by the window of her living room, looking across the drab backyards to the warm lights of her neighbors. She'd turned on the hall light when she came home, thrown hat and coat on the couch and sunk into the easy chair, holding the company check for $1200 in flaccid fingers. Somewhere in her purse was another check for $500, from Dr. Innisperg, "to cover Christmas and birth-day presents . . . Use it for fare on one of those freighters that go from port to port without itin-erary . . ."

In the cab, he'd made it sound easy: "Inocula-tions tomorrow; the company will arrange pass-port; I'll give you enough letters of introduction to come out your ears! Leave your apartment keys with me: we've Roberts and Horgan, who always have someone coming for conferences or reassignment . . . let 'em use your place! Cheaper than a hotel and a damn sight more comfortable—plus, our guys won't steal anything."

"They won't dare, if *you* check the inventory." Megan laughed—but of course it wouldn't be that easy.

Clothes, suitcases, arrange to hold the mail, alert the superintendent, clean and defrost the fridge, get rid of food . . . just thinking of all the chores was ex-hausting, but there was worse. The pretty clothes bought for New York and Bob would be useless on a freighter; high-heeled pumps would be worse than useless for sightseeing. No one knew how slim her bank balance was; everyone assumed she must have some reserve, even if not enough for six months with-out salary. Well, now it would have to come out. Uncle Joe Ames would be shocked to learn that Sid Royce's daughter was a silly fool, but he'd lend her anything she wanted—and tear up the IOU as soon as she signed it.

How much would she need? Megan got up, sway-ing with sudden giddiness when she reached for the lamp switch. "Nine thirty? I need something to eat, must be sensible . . ." she thought. "I must be a good girl in return for all this help."

Facing the expensive goodies in her pantry, Megan rebelled. There was a hundred bucks' worth of food in those cans bought for dinner *à deux* with Bob. She would use it up! She began fixing soup and crackers first. While the packet turned into broth, Megan fixed snails the way *she* liked them (plenty of garlic), spread the remains of the cooking wine over stale French bread, concocted a salad, and set half a bottle of wine to chill.

She sat on the kitchen stool and consumed the soup, after which she felt stronger, but sleepy. She fought it off by changing to her company housecoat and bathing her face in cold water. Coming back to the living room, she stood in the archway. "If I never saw this room again, would I care?" she wondered. Suppose she kept the family heirlooms and abandoned everything else for what it would fetch?

It was definitely an Idea. While she set the table, lit candles, opened the wine, and served her dinner, Megan considered. If she was going away for six months, why come back to the reminder of her folly? Dr. Innisperg had said he'd rent the place furnished to Madison Oil execs, and Megan had a hunch he'd pay the rent himself if there wasn't a tenant—but in six months the lease would be up.

She decided to ask Uncle Joe. The super and the apartment management were kindly disposed to tenants; she would ask them to sell her furnishings, with Uncle Joe to supervise. There'd be enough to repay any loan he made her, surely, and Megan would return to start fresh in every way.

Savoring the garlicky snails and wine, Megan began to feel almost cheerful. Look forward, not back— and the Lord helps those who help themselves . . . The telephone rang. Megan jumped slightly, tilting the forkful of salad into its bowl. Nearly eleven? It could only be Dr. Innisperg making sure she was okay. She picked up the phone and said, warmly, "Hello, don't worry! I'm fine!"

There was a startled pause. "I'm delighted to hear it, Miss Royce," said a strange masculine voice.

Megan gasped. "Who are you?"

"Who did you think I was?"

"Dr. Innisperg," she said dazedly.

"Ah? Well, no, I am not—although I am sure he is a most worthy gentleman."

"He certainly *is*," Megan retorted vigorously. "He's the chief of foreign exploration for Madison Oil, and my boss, and *anybody* knows who Dr. Innisperg is, for heaven's sake."

"So I am an illiterate nobody, Miss Royce," he chuckled.

Megan gulped and thought of the horrid degenerates who telephone feminine listings at random . . . "Who are you, please?"

"Lorenzo di Frecchia," he said, "and in a roundabout way I have your name from Dr. Ames. I apologize for calling so late, but, frankly, I was afraid you might make other arrangements."

Now Megan caught the tiny foreign accent in his gentle tenor voice—but he had mentioned Uncle Joe. "Arrangements?"

"For your trip abroad. Are you occupied," he asked politely, "or may I explain to you?"

"How did you know I—might go abroad?"

"My sister Mrs. Upjohn goes to Dr. Ames today," di Frecchia outlined rapidly. "Her examination is interrupted by a call from your employers. Dr. Ames explains the delay and mentions a little of your situation: you've had a serious operation; you need

14

six months' rest; you should get completely away, go abroad—but there is no family, no money. You are alone in the world; that is correct?"

"My mother—died a year ago, yes."

"So, you are alone, and that is sad," he went on briskly, "but when my sister mentions this at dinner, *I* see it is a perfect solution, Miss Royce.

"I have been at wits' ends," he said earnestly, "but if you agree, all is settled for both of us. You wish to go abroad; money is a problem. My mother also wishes to go abroad, and she does not like to travel alone—*not* a question of a nurse or courier, you understand? Merely a traveling companion as far as Paris and to see her comfortably onto the plane for Milano, where my brother will meet her.

"And for this, we will pay round-trip airplane fare, first class," he finished simply. "Would you consider it?"

"Well—I suppose so," Megan said hesitantly, "but if she doesn't need a nurse, why isn't the stewardess enough?"

"There will be four hours to wait at Orly," he confided, and chuckled disarmingly, "and my mother is Mrs. Lucius Waldron. I may not know this Dr. Innisperg, but I suspect you have heard of Mrs. Lucius Waldron—and that is a sad commentary on our times, no?"

"I'm afraid so," Megan admitted, "Filthy-rich society is better known than distinguished petroleum geologist."

Mr. di Frecchia laughed heartily. "You put it well, Miss Royce. But," he sobered down, "it is a problem. My mother has decided to go to Italy next Monday, she decrees someone must accompany her, and as it happens, Monday is not convenient for either my sister or myself. If she would go Saturday, Luisa could go; if she would wait till Wednesday, I am free. But no! It must be Monday; who knows why?" His voice was a shrug. "So: my mother is rich, she can indulge her whims—and occasionally she likes to be stubborn over some tiny matter. She *will* leave Monday; she *will* have a companion. Will you go with her, Miss Royce? It is only to sit beside her, to talk or be silent as she wishes, and to wait with her at Orly until she is on the plane to Milano."

"If that's *all*," Megan said slowly, "because you do understand I've been seriously ill? If anything went wrong, I'd be no physical use whatever."

"Nothing will go wrong," he assured her. "It is only to avert boredom for an elderly woman who is rich and a little spoiled." He laughed affectionately. "A few hours only, and a comfortable solution for both of us. What do you say?"

Only twelve hours . . . even if Mrs. Waldron were an old witch, how bad could it be, for heaven's sake? Round-trip, first-class air ticket? Megan thought rapidly. If she cashed in the return half, even after freighter passage, she'd have about $600 extra—perhaps she'd have no need to borrow anything. "All right," she said. "When would you like me to come for an interview?"

"Oh, that is not necessary."

"But how do you know I'll be suitable?"

Mr. di Frecchia laughed comfortably. "By your voice. My mother will not care what you look like, so long as your voice is pleasing." He laughed again. "I can picture you, Miss Royce: your voice says you are young, well-bred, the typical chic American secretary, *and* you have a sense of humor . . . but if you are six feet tall, two hundred pounds, with

16

spectacles and flat feet"—his tone held suppressed amusement—"well—I confess I shall be surprised . . . but it will not matter to my mother, so long as your voice does not offend her ears.

"In any case, she is visiting friends out of town," he finished. "I must have a traveling companion for her by six P.M. next Monday. Will you agree?"

"How can I resist?" she said, suddenly lighthearted. "You are the answer to a prayer, Mr. di Frecchia."

"It is vice versa, I assure you!" He sighed with relief, then he became brisk and businesslike . . .

It was nearly midnight before Megan cradled the phone and looked at the instructions she had automatically noted in shorthand: flight number, departure-arrival hours, be ready for limousine here at 3:30, and pick up her tickets from baggage clerk at the Carlyle . . . disregard excess baggage costs, and any price difference on the return ticket to be reimbursed if she didn't come back from Paris . . .

Megan picked up her glass of wine, stood twisting it thoughtfully in her fingers, and finally raised it in a mocking salute. "To *me!*" she said aloud, and drained the glass. She had an almost superstitious sense of Fate taking a hand, as she made coffee and washed up the dinner dishes. Everything that had seemed impossible a few hours ago was reversed by this one stroke of good luck . . . but it would be only the beginning, she thought happily. "Out of the depths and up to the heights; put your trust in the Lord, and the way always opens."

For the first time in months, Megan could look forward to tomorrow, and tomorrow, and tomorrow . . . which somehow made it possible also to look back without anguish. Actually, she was fortunate that Bob was gone! "I always wanted to live abroad for a while," she told herself. "If Bob hadn't walked out, I'd be stuck in Los Angeles, right this minute, instead of going to Europe . . . learning everything, and preparing for a glamorous, responsible career!"

Sitting over the coffee cup with a celebration glass of Cherry Heering, Megan planned dreamily . . . laughing at her grandiose concepts, because she would still need to count pennies. But it cost nothing to let her fancy travel, and some of the dreams might come true. It was going to be fun to see which ones! In her soul, Megan *knew* that the next six months were going to be right, smooth all the way; nothing would go wrong; and every act, every decision, would be correct.

"Roses, roses, all the way," she said aloud, and was overtaken by a tremendous yawn. "Ooooh, *bed!* To-morrow is another day. . . ."

CHAPTER TWO

"And you are the good girl who will keep me company?" Mrs. Waldron's voice was deeply warm and clear, yet no more beautiful than the woman herself. Megan could barely restrain herself from staring at the elegant figure before her: dark eyes, dark hair winged with white at the temples, and a smile of compelling sweetness.

"Yes, Mrs. Waldron."

"Charming, attractive," the older woman murmured, flicking a practiced glance up and down—the sort of glance to make one wonder, "Does my slip show; are my heels run over; am I wearing too much jewelry?" But Mrs. Waldron's eyes were kindly. "Not pretty," she stated, "but sometimes beautiful, I shouldn't wonder. What's your name, my dear?"

"Megan Royce."

"It suits you," Mrs. Waldron decided. "Yes. You are not ordinary; you can carry off an unusual name." She nodded with satisfaction. "I think we shall like each other. I shall ask a great many impertinent questions, which you will answer because you are a sweet-natured child—and I shall tell you a great many extremely boring stories, to which you will listen with apparent interest, because you are a sweet-natured child," she remarked mischievously, "but I think we will both enjoy it."

"I'm sure *I* shall!" Megan smiled. Glancing about at bellboys and maids quietly scurrying about to dispatch luggage under the supervision of a Very Superior Person, who was efficiently checking a list by the door, she asked, "Will your son see us off? I'm curious to meet him, after the snow job he did on me!"

"My *son?*"

"He hired me." Megan faltered uncertainly at the sudden stiffness in Mrs. Waldron's face. "Is there some mistake? I understood I was to accompany you to Paris, merely to see you aboard the plane to Milan in return for a round-trip, first-class air ticket—but if there's anything you dislike in those arrangements . . ." Megan quietly extended the airline folder.

"No, there's nothing I dislike about you." The voice was casual, but Megan could see fingers clenched on a chair back, bloodless from . . . what? Anger? Surprise? "I thought you were engaged by my daughter."

"Oh? Well, in a way I was," Megan said with relief. "She heard of me from Dr. Ames, and when she told Mr. di Frecchia, *he* telephoned me, last Monday night. If you think it's a bit flighty of me to agree," Megan smiled, "I did check Dr. Ames the next day—and of course, anyone knows who you are, Mrs. Waldron."

"Anyone and everyone," Mrs. Waldron answered cynically. "So Cesare was—concerned for me?"

"He said his name was Lorenzo di Frecchia." Megan felt bewildered, but apparently it made sense, though it was still surprising. Mrs. Waldron's hands relaxed.

"I thought he was out of town," she murmured, with a flicker of dark eyebrows, turning away as a maid bustled forward.

"*C'est tout, M'dame, nous sommes prêtes.*"

"*Merci* . . . Elise, this is Miss Royce, who comes with us." Mrs. Waldron turned gracefully to settle the mink stole draped over her shoulders and receive her delicate suede handbag and fresh white gloves. They'd be filthy in half an hour, Megan thought absently, exchanging polite smiles with Elise; but presumably if you were rich, you just—threw them away? In the final stir of departure, she forgot the odd reaction to her employment. Now, this minute, began Megan's new life. She meant to make the most of every second.

Money *does* make a difference, Megan realized—not special privilege, but recognition and courtesy. The people at the passport desk, the boarding agent, the stewardesses—all knew Mrs. Waldron, as she moved leisurely toward her seat, smiling graciously, saying, "How nice to see you again. This is Miss Royce, who travels with me . . ."

"Miss Royce! Ah, there is something for you . . ." A white orchid, with a Bon Voyage card signed by everyone in the Department. Megan smiled mistily. "From the people I work with. Do you mind if I wear it?"

"What else would you do with it? It is not a salad, after all. So, there are people who love you?" as Megan pinned the flower to her suit. "I had the impression, I don't know why, that you were quite alone and friendless."

Why this emphasis on her being alone? "My father died ten years ago, my mother last spring—and a few months later I was jilted," Megan said evenly. "I had a serious appendectomy, and I've no money left, but of course I have friends. The company gave me six months' leave and enough money to live simply, and my job is waiting, I'm sorry if I was supposed to be a charity case; I'm not, really."

She had again the odd sense that her explanation was satisfactory, yet did not fit some preconceived idea. "No, no, not charity, I assure you," Mrs. Waldron murmured, absently, and relapsed into silence, while Megan sat uneasily. Was she here under false pretenses? Not of her doing, yet why hadn't the man asked? The older woman's lips twitched suddenly. "Don't look so distressed, child. 'Renzo couldn't have pleased me better if he'd chosen you in person." She patted Megan's hand gently. "A pity he didn't. His loss, I fear . . . Ah, we're off. Is your seat belt secure?"

The thrilling lights of New York were far behind, the superb French dinner consumed, and there was nothing to see but darkness split by stars, but Megan was wide awake. "Sit by the window, my dear. I shall doze for a while. I'll advise you to do likewise, but you won't. You'll stare at the stars, making impossible plans . . . and you'll be *dead* tomorrow!" Mrs. Waldron chuckled. "I, on the other hand, shall be fresh as a daisy, but longitude will catch up with you shortly after waving good-bye to the Milan plane!

"Never mind! I did the same at your age, although it was trains in those days. I remember staying awake all night, on the Orient Express—nothing to see, but imagining the hills and valleys, the people asleep in darkened villages." She smiled reminiscently. "When you are young, you're so damned afraid you'll miss something—and when you are old, you'd give anything for the time you wasted on ephemera."

"*Si jeunesse savait, si vieillesse pouvait,*" Megan murmured involuntarily.

Mrs. Waldron's eyes flew open. "*Vous parlez français?*"

"*Seulement de l'école; je manque des mots, vous savez.*"

"*L'accent est pur, tout de même.* Only French, or other languages, too?"

"Two years of college Italian," Megan admitted, startled by the keen glance. "One reason I'm to be in Europe: to learn colloquial speech, so I can handle a foreign office."

"Ah, now I understand: 'Renzo hired you because your French will be useful at Orly."

Megan frowned uncertainly. "I don't think he asked about languages at all."

"So he does not know you are a linguist? How surprised he will be to learn your usefulness!" Mrs. Waldron laughed softly, while Megan protested, "I'm not a linguist, only a few words, for heaven's sake!" Mrs. Waldron was still amused, as at some private joke. "Don't be too modest, my dear; I feel sure your few words will be all I need. Now, if you will ring for the stewardess, I shall have a pillow, please . . ."

Megan stared at the stars, but she was more occupied with the strange undercurrent than with beautiful dreams. It was sheer idle curiosity, of course. Without egotism, she knew she was being more than satisfactory as a companion, actually making the trip pleasant and amusing for Mrs. Waldron, by her descriptions of the office personnel: all so different, so brilliant, yet so childlike beneath their scholarly achievements.

Mrs. Waldron had practically guffawed over Dr. Zhondek's struggle with the English language and was enchanted by Megan's report of a trilingual debate between Johanssen, Zhondek, and a visiting Spaniard —in which nobody understood anyone, until Dr. Innisperg arrived.

"Talk, or be silent, as she wishes"; but Mrs. Waldron wished Megan to talk. Looking at the Big Dipper absently, Megan thought, "I'm practically Scheherazade!"

And yet, and yet . . . every so often the odd wariness? Megan had meant to consult a Social Register; there hadn't been time, so she literally knew nothing of Mrs. Lucius Waldron beyond the obvious fact that she'd once been married to an Italian and produced children . . . but how many? Mrs. Upjohn, Lorenzo, Cesare . . . but there was a son to meet the Milan plane.

Slowly Megan pieced together the reactions, until she finally thought she understood. Mrs. Waldron was rich, spoiled, nearly seventy; her children had fed her a sob story of poor, penniless, orphaned Megan, "rehabilitation of a sad case!" If they'd only briefed her, first, and *said* they wanted someone to supervise unobtrusively! Instead, she'd given the whole thing away even before they were on the plane and let Mrs. Waldron realize her family had put one over on Mama! She'd been sporting enough to go along with it, for Megan's sake, but Megan suspected naughtily that the di Frecchia kids would get their heads handed to them as soon as Mama got them alone!

Ten to one, Mrs. Waldron had never asked for a companion; she had probably even refused an escort —so her children had pulled a fast one . . . on Megan, as well. That was why there was no personal interview: to establish Megan's innocence and absolve her of complicity in the gentle family plot! It was rather nice that Mrs. Waldron's family loved her so dearly, Megan decided drowsily—and in spite of herself, she fell asleep . . . to be roused by the stewardess. "We land in thirty minutes, ma'mselle; fasten your belt, please."

Blearily, Megan's eyes met Mrs. Waldron's amused twinkle. "I warned you! Never mind; only four hours before bed. Where are you staying?"

"I don't know." Megan stifled a yawn and shook herself briskly. "I've a list of *pensions*. I'll get a cab after you leave and see what looks promising."

Mrs. Waldron was deeply disturbed, almost angry. "No reservation? Where had you this list, from former patrons? *No*? But this is *impossible* in Lorenzo, to send a young girl into a foreign city, alone, with no arrangements!"

"Please, you mustn't blame him. I was only engaged for the trip, and I was very generously paid," Megan said earnestly. "There's no reason he should be responsible for my hotel reservation. He probably thought my plans were already made . . . and they would have been, if there'd been time."

"He should have inquired," Mrs. Waldron stated with regal finality. "Never mind; we will settle it while we wait." She was suddenly superb, formal, in command . . . shaking hands with stewardesses, leaving folded bills behind, confiding a small envelope "for Captain Harmon—a delightful flight . . ."

It wasn't over, yet. "I dislike being pushed," Mrs.

Waldron said. She and Megan sat calmly while the stampede passed and vanished. Then, and then only, Mrs. Waldron rose, adjusted the fur stole and smoothed the fresh white gloves Elise had brought from her seat at the rear of the plane. Then, with Megan behind her, she made her way majestically to the landing steps. Halfway down, the fashionable spike heel caught, twisted, and broke at the shank, while Mrs. Waldron dropped her handbag and caught herself breathlessly by the handrail . . . dangling like a rag doll, a half inch from plunging head first to the bottom of the steps!

The landing officer bounded upward, amid a chorus of feminine shrieks from stewardesses above, and Elise promptly dropped everything to fling her hands dramatically over her eyes, moaning. One arm bracing Mrs. Waldron, Megan spoke sharply, authoritative from automatic reflex: *"Tais-toi, Elise! Retrouve la pochette de Madame à l'instant—làbas . . ."*

Heaven knows how much money might be in that handbag, let alone the contents of the slim jewel case Elise had dropped. Megan kept an eagle eye on both items, while the steward assisted Mrs. Waldron to the ground, and Elise scurried to pick up bag, jewel case, extra coat, and magazines. She was totally disorganized, and tears streamed down her face, while she thrust everything at Megan and devoted herself to her mistress.

"I'm quite all right; merely wrenched my ankle." Mrs. Waldron limped forward on the steward's arm to the private lounge for VIPs, where she pleasantly but firmly dismissed everyone but Megan. "I cannot stand fussing," she murmured, closing her eyes.

Megan stared at her dubiously: ghastly white, obviously shaken up, and wincing with pain. "I shan't

fuss," she said gently, "but do lie down, put the
foot up, and rest it . . . you've four hours, after all. Let
me get a pillow, perhaps coffee and a croissant?"

"What a good child you are!" The dark eyes were
almost apologetic. "That was so stupid of me . . . yes,
coffee would be pleasant."

"This was exactly what was *not* supposed to happen," Megan thought dryly, going in search of Elise.
Oh, well, a wrenched ankle was minor compared to,
say, a heart attack . . . but after a few minutes of
French red tape, a heart attack seemed preferable!

Transport *petit déjeuner* to the private lounge?
Impossible. It would not be possible to have pillows
until the concierge arrived at 7 A.M.—nor bandages
and rubbing alcohol until the nurse unlocked her supplies at 8. Most of all, it was not possible, *absolument
défendu,* that anyone should open Madame's luggage
for a fresh pair of shoes.

"Oh, no?" said Megan. It took her half an hour
to interview all witnesses, after which she hunted up
the Airport Chief and gently stated that *if* Mrs.
Waldron were made comfortable, it might be possible
to persuade her not to prosecute.

"Prosecute? *Mais pourquoi?*"

"Shoes," Megan said tersely. "She needs a pair. Also
something to eat and some rubbing alcohol." She
eyed him provocatively and made use of her dimple.
"You can't *possibly* suspect Mrs. Lucius Waldron of
secreting illicit gems or narcotics in her shoes—*can
you?*"

He chuckled helplessly. "No, we do not, Ma'm-
selle. *Alors,* send the maid and the keys; I arrange
it."

By the time Megan got back to the lounge, bearing shoes, sustenance, and a bottle of white wine,

Mrs. Waldron was propped against pillows, her ankle on a *fauteuil*. The lounge custodian was now on duty, whisking about in floods of French ineptitude.

"Here we are," Megan said cheerily, settling the tray on Mrs. Waldron's lap; but inwardly she was appalled by the strained white face, the pleading, exhausted eyes. "*Je vous prie*," she said firmly to the concierge, "*silence, Madame s'est donneé une entourse au coup-de-pied, c'est tout—mais il faut qu'elle reste un peu.*"

"*Aaaah, pauvre madame! Oui, oui, je comprends!*"

"Oh, bless you, bless you," Mrs. Waldron murmured faintly, sipping her coffee. "I thought I should go mad!"

"Yes, one does." Megan eyed the injured ankle dubiously. It seemed alarmingly puffed. "I couldn't get any liniment before eight, when the nurse arrives —so I brought white wine. I thought you might smell a bit odd, but it *is* alcohol . . . only shouldn't we have a doctor?"

"*No!* I will *not* have unknown doctors; always mountains of molehills because I am Mrs. Waldron. It's only a sprain, not broken. Yes, it's agonizingly painful, but it can wait until I reach Milan and a doctor I know."

"All right," Megan soothed, and grinned wickedly. "How do you feel about a light massage with *vin blanc?*"

"You're right, it smells a bit peculiar," Mrs. Waldron chuckled a few minutes later, "but it feels extremely good."

"Let's hope there's no gossip column snoop," Megan giggled irrepressibly, continuing the light strokes up and down, over and around, dousing the ankle with more wine. "Oh, can't see the item! "What international millionairess was assisted, tottering, to the Milano plane, surrounded by an aura of octane high enough to clear the Alps under her own power . . . ?"

Mrs. Waldron snorted and threw back her head, laughing heartily. "Megan, you're a delight!" She stared at Megan, suddenly serious. "Have we begun to be friends?"

"Of course! Nothing was ever nicer than traveling with you!"

"The test of friendship, as separate from mere acquaintance, is the privilege of asking favors," Mrs. Waldron said, slowly. "If we are friends, I shall ask a favor, Megan."

"Well—if I can . . ."

"Don't simply put me on the plane to Milano, *come with me?*" Mrs. Waldron shifted, pulling up to lean forward compellingly. "You said you'd no reservations, no plans," she said urgently. "Does it matter if you start in Italy instead of France? I confess: *I dread the trip alone.* I know I should not ask; you've been really sick—but if you could . . . I beg you, Megan!"

Megan felt hypnotized by the pleading dark eyes, while her fingers gently resumed the light massage. Why *not* start in Italy?

"I shall pay for the ticket, but more than that—you're meant first to rest and relax. Come to Vellanti with me, as a guest for a few weeks? Save your money, my dear; look at the Lake Como and listen to the olives growing!"

This was all part of the dreamlike rightness of this trip, Megan thought vaguely: living expenses and fare could be saved in return for assisting a woman she *liked.* "Of course I'll come with you!" Megan literally suppressed tears at the untensing of Mrs. Waldron's face. "We'd better confirm your reservation and get me a seat . . ."

There was not, of course, a seat on the Milan flight. Megan debated briefly. If all else failed, she would dump Elise and hope to charm Mrs. Waldron's seat mate into exchanging for a window seat—but first she would pull rank! "*C'est moi encore,*" she said sadly, and flashed a wicked grin at the Airport Chief. "*Alors,* all that is needed to settle this affair is a ticket entitling *me* to occupy Seat 24B on the Milan flight . . ."

He spluttered slightly, but in the end Megan got it—plus a languishing glance, a kiss on the hand, and a sighed "*Pas au revoir—à bientôt!*" Trotting back to the lounge, Megan thought, "So far so good," but impasse lurked ahead.

There was not a single rolling chair available in the whole of Orly Airport. All, but *all,* had been bespoke for pilgrims to Lourdes. Megan admitted defeat, marshaled Elise and the lounge concierge (with a *douceur* of impressive proportions) to get Mrs. Waldron from lounge to boarding line . . . and there was still what appeared a half-mile walk to the plane.

Mrs. Waldron clung white-faced to Elise, the custodian vanished, and the boarding officer was sour-faced and uncooperative. Such porters as were in evidence were obviously sweating under a press of business beyond the usual. Megan stared about helplessly, but with growing determination; then she had it. "How proud are you?" she asked with detachment. "You can't walk that far; we can't carry you; there are no rolling chairs or husky porters; so—be my guest?" She gestured to the waiting baggage truck, piled high. "A tidy space, just here, exactly suited to your sit-upon."

Mrs. Waldron stared at Megan blankly, but before she could say anything, there was a volcanic eruption at the boarding desk. Instinctively, Megan looked over her shoulder at a slender, dark-haired man flourishing tickets, practically dancing up and down with rage. So that's who was dumped? It couldn't, Megan decided contemptuously, have happened to a nicer person!

"Help me up, Megan!" Mrs. Waldron urged. "Clever girl, to think of this—but quickly, the driver is coming . . ." Yes, Megan realized, a man in dirty overalls was sliding behind the wheel. "Allez-oop!" she said blithely, and between a jump and a heave, Mrs. Waldron was on the truck just as it rolled forward.

Glancing back, Megan saw the boarding gate rolling shut, while the man whose seat she'd commandeered stared furiously at the plane, his fingers twisting the airline folder convulsively. If looks could kill . . . Megan shivered involuntarily, as the gate clanged shut . . . and whirled in sudden memory: Mrs. Waldron was still sitting trustfully among the baggage!

Megan picked up her heels and sped forward, yelling "Wait!" Already the grapnels were in place, the maw of the airplane was open, the driver was leaning to the decoupling buttons, and the luggage rack was about to ascend . . . "*Quick*, get *down*, Mrs. Waldron!"

"Is he gone?" she whispered faintly, as Megan pulled her forcibly from the truck, braced her, and turned her to the landing steps.

"Is who gone?" Megan asked, distractedly. "Please

—they're ready to close the plane . . . Steward! Help Madame, please."

Instant sensation: "Signora Waldron, we wait . . . but what has happened? Tchk, tchk, Ernesto—carry the signora, *subito!* Signorina Royce? Ah, yes, you go with the signora . . . quickly please . . . fasten the belt at once, please . . ."

Twenty minutes later, Paris was far behind. Megan had the aisle seat, and Elise stood timidly behind them, *"M'dame désire quelqu'chose?"*

"A glass of water. A proper glass, not a paper cup." Mrs. Waldron looked at Megan. "Well. It was an adventure, no?"

"Never to my dying day," Megan stated with detachment, "shall I forget the sight of *you;* perched regally upon the baggage truck, bowling genteelly over the tarmac," she began to chuckle, "with a Black Watch plaid zipper bag behind you . . . and the most dreadful little man, making a tantrum because I bumped him . . ."

"Bumped?"

Megan nodded, half crying in amusement. "There wasn't a seat; I had to go to the Chief . . . and when I said, *'C'est moi encore . . .'* " Megan choked, "he took one look and gave me *anything.* After your shoes, he was glad to get rid of me."

"Shoes?"

"How d'you think I got them? They were in bond —but I promised you wouldn't sue!" Megan pantomimed naïveté, until Mrs. Waldron suddenly sank back, laughing helplessly.

"Oh, good heavens, I never thought." She laughed quietly and laid a warm hand on Megan's. "You clever little witch! How glad I am you're with me, my dear!"

"Even more, if you could have seen what was supposed to be in this seat! You wouldn't have liked him at all!"

"I'm sure I shouldn't," Mrs. Waldron said after a moment. "Ah, thank you, Elise," she said, leaning forward to take the glass of water. "*C'est tout, merci.*" She sat back, sipping the water and gazing from the window. "I do not offer this window seat," she said suddenly, "because it means more to me than to you. This is Dijon—in the distance, Besançon—we come to Geneva and the Alps . . . Do you care for mountains?"

"I never saw any but the Eastern ridges."

"They are pretty," the soft voice was polite but disparaging, "but even your Rockies cannot compare to *les Alpes . . .*" She glanced at Megan. "Why do you frown?"

"Adding two and two," Megan smiled ruefully. "You're not American, but Italian, aren't you?"

"*Si, certamente.* You did not know?"

Megan shook her head. "I meant to look you up, but I forgot."

"Ah? Well, I was born Contessa Giulia Vellanti; I married Prince Uberto di Frecchia. After his death, I married Lucius Waldron." The dark eyes studied Megan somberly. "*Io sono vedova ricca . . .* and you do not know this?"

"Only the rich widow part, not the background. Why would I? I don't live in your world."

"But you would like to?"

"Not really. It would be nice to be able always to pay the bills, but I don't mind earning my living."

"Wouldn't you like furs, jewels, Paris gowns, handmade underwear?" Mrs. Waldron insisted.

Megan pursed her lips thoughtfully. "Emeralds

33

and ermine, and you worry about burglars . . . you can buy Paris copies for a third of the price—and who sees your underwear?" Megan smiled, but the dark eyes were still oddly intent, compelling her to amplify her remarks. "You think of such things because you've always had them, but they aren't part of my life. Actually," Megan said slowly, "I don't much want to marry them. I'd feel like a fish out of water, forever straining to fit a life I wasn't trained to live."

Mrs. Waldron turned to the window again, while Megan thought fleetingly of the life she'd expected to live with Bob . . . but there'd be another man. Did she want wealth? Not, she thought instantly, if it meant traveling with a paid companion, or the constant wariness she sensed in Giulia Vellanti di Frecchia Waldron!

"Ah, now we begin to see," Mrs. Waldron breathed yearningly. "Look, Megan!" She settled into the corner of her seat, imperiously pulling Megan forward, to rest against her shoulder. "See—that is Neuchâtel . . . soon Geneva and Mont Blanc, we go a little south . . . down and over *les Alpes Maritimes,* toward Torino, and finally Milano. . . ." She was speaking Italian now, but leaning toward the window breathlessly, nearly cheek to cheek with her. Megan understood enough.

Never had she dreamed of such majesty, such sheer total beauty, the intermittent flash of sun against ice, the quick glimpses of valley villages shadowed by the mountains, an occasional impertinent sunbeam slanting arrogantly downward to strike a random tree, a wooden chalet, a small pasture in which cows grazed. From the plane floating lazily through the heights, the view was miniature, precise

. . . like a display of toys in a Christmas window at F.A.O. Schwarz or Lord & Taylor.

Megan felt overwhelmed by good fortune, the marvelous luck of this flight . . . and for nothing beyond a bit of ingenuity, to get shoes, make someone comfortable. "*Bellissimo*," she murmured half to herself. "*E sorprendente, oltre sogno.*"

"*Si*, they are beyond dreams," Mrs. Waldron agreed softly, when Mont Blanc was finally lost to sight. "So—you like my mountains?"

"Yes." Megan drew a long breath and pulled back to her own seat. "That says it; there aren't words."

Mrs. Waldron laughed. "*E vero!*" she agreed. "Ring for the stewardess and ask Elise to help me to the washroom, please? I shall leave you to reminisce. No," as Megan protested, "it's an old story to Elise, my dear. Slip across to my seat—not much to see, but enjoy what there is."

Fifteen minutes later Megan agreed there was not much to see, slid into the aisle to get herself a glass of water, and faced Mrs. Waldron returning from the lavatory, her head turned to speak to Elise behind her.

She was entirely erect and elegant in the coral wool travel suit, stepping forward on the spike-heeled pumps (size 5AAA) that had cost Megan such machinations at Orly . . . walking sure-footed as a chamois in that faint dip and tilt of the plane, *with no trace of a limp* . . .

CHAPTER THREE

Megan whirled back to her seat, gulping in bewilderment. "Why?" she wondered. "If there's nothing wrong with her ankle, what am I doing here?" Megan felt certain, now, that Mrs. Waldron had never needed nor wanted a traveling companion; Megan had been thrust upon her and gracefully endured . . . and Megan *had* proved useful for those few hours at Orly; but if Mrs. Waldron's ankle was so recovered within this short time for her to cope with an airplane in flight, it must have been nearly all right before they ever left Orly.

Why, then, had she prolonged the companionship she'd only suffered because there was no help for it? Rich quixotism, Megan decided humbly: "I did help pass the time pleasantly; she liked me; she wanted to give me a bonus but knew I wouldn't accept money —but of course I'd never abandon her with a bum ankle."

"*Ma'mselle!*" Elise hissed importantly, and Megan slid into the aisle, poker-faced, observing Mrs. Waldron's halting progress back to her seat, where she collapsed with a sigh of anguish and closed her eyes.

A magnificent performance! Elise must be in on it, too. Beneath her solicitous inquiries, Megan won-

dered amusedly how long Mrs. Waldron would main-
tain the injured ankle caper?

The engines were barely stopped, the door barely
opened on landing steps, when a man thrust vigorously through the disembarking passengers to halt
beside Megan. He leaned across, ignoring her, with
his hand stretched to Mrs. Waldron. *"Mama!"* he said
gleefully.

"Cesare, come sta?" Mrs. Waldron's face lit with
affection, while Megan surveyed him covertly. He
wasn't much to look at, she decided, aside from
his mother's magnificent dark eyes and thick, wavy
hair . . . but he was loaded with a positively indecent
amount of charm! His deep voice was alternately
softly seductive and ebullient, as he engaged Mrs.
Waldron in a rapid interchange of Italian beyond
Megan's comprehension. . . . There was a fluid grace
in his body, as he somehow swept the people from
the seats ahead and knelt in the vacant space, leaning over the back to hold Mrs. Waldron's hand ca-
ressingly.

Even without understanding more than one word
in ten, Megan responded to his infectious pleasure,
noting Mrs. Waldron's equal pleasure, until Elise
stood beside them. *"Madame veut partir?"* There was
another minor Old Home Week while Cesare di
Frecchia greeted her enthusiastically, but now he
was speaking in French, and Megan could follow his
outrageous compliments, which reduced Elise to un-
controllable giggles. When finally he compared her
to a dove bearing roses, both Megan and Mrs.
Waldron burst into laughter. For the first time, Cesare
looked at Megan.

"We are not very polite, but of course you know
Miss Royce?" Mrs. Waldron asked.

"I confess I have not that honor," he smiled, extending a hand. "How do you do?"

"You did not know?" Mrs. Waldron raised her eyebrows in surprise. "Miss Royce is the traveling companion 'Renzo chose for me in New York." At the convulsive grasp of her hand, Megan nearly cried out, but in a split second he'd abandoned her fingers as if rejecting contamination. "She was only supposed to see me onto this plane," Mrs. Waldron went on placidly. "Now, where *is* my handbag? Elise, do you have it? Oh, no—it has fallen . . .

"But I was stupid: I twisted my ankle at Orly, and Miss Royce was persuaded to come on to Milano." Mrs. Waldron smiled at Megan. "And now she will visit us for a few weeks. Shall we go?"

In silence they filed from the plane. Cesare brushed aside the landing steward and calmly picked his mother up bodily, to carry her down the steps and across the strip to the waiting limousine, while Megan and Elise followed. Staring at the tall figure striding ahead, Megan was stupefied by his instant recoil at the mention of Lorenzo. . . . Yet Mrs. Waldron had equally recoiled in New York at the possibility Cesare had hired Megan. The undercurrent was back, still incomprehensible—except that Megan was not only shaken by his dislike, but a bit wary.

When they arrived at the car, Elise hopped into the front seat while a chauffeur opened the rear door, and Cesare set down his mother. Megan stood uncertain and uncomfortable at the vehement tirade he was voicing, obviously protesting Megan's presence.

Mrs. Waldron ignored him briefly, to address the chauffeur, Ugo, who apparently was a family fixture despite his dour face. "No, we will not send the car back for Megan; she comes with me," Mrs. Waldron finally stated, climbing briskly into the car and establishing herself in the corner. "Sit in the center if you please, Megan."

"Whoooo, she's mad as hops! She even forgot to limp," Megan thought naughtily, and she nipped past Cesare's furious face, with only a bland "Excuse me . . ." Cesare had no alternative but to sink into the other corner in grim silence.

Even hemmed in, Megan caught tiny glimpses of Milan through the traffic. She'd almost forgotten she was a buffer state when Cesare's deep voice delivered a few fulminating comments . . . and this time, Megan got the gist. He'd looked forward to a private chat with Mama; he wanted to show her something (he lost Megan briefly here); and now all, but *tutti*, was ruined by 'Renzo's *petite-amie* so cleverly foisted on Mama . . .

"I am *not!*" Megan said indignantly, entirely forgetting she was an involuntary eavesdropper. "I never met your brother in my life . . . and I'm sorry I ruined your surprise, whatever it is, except I'm not really sorry, because your mother's been traveling for hours, and she's tired, for heaven's sake. Let her have a good night's rest and show her tomorrow; haven't you *any* sense?"

"Not much, I fear, but don't be too hard on him, Megan," Mrs. Waldron pleaded with suppressed amusement, while Cesare's face was aghast. "Yes, she speaks very nice French and a bit of Italian—and it seems 'Renzo didn't know this either."

"I—beg your pardon, Miss Royce," he said stiffly. Megan inclined her head slightly and turned to look from the other window. They were away from the city, running through suburbs-leading into real country. "Monza . . . Canto, shortly, then Como," Mrs. Waldron murmured. "We pass Villa d'Este; you shall see it another day . . . Ah, there are new cottages at Szirbino. You did not tell me!"

"Part of what I meant to show you." Cesare shrugged sulkily, but in a few minutes he was kneeling by the window, eagerly pointing out this and that, all smiles again. "How volatile can you be?" Megan wondered, but at least the rest of the drive was more comfortable.

When finally they drove through imposing gates, opened by a beaming guard equipped with a furious mustache and a spouse in native costume, curtseying, smiling, thrusting roses into Mrs. Waldron's hands, Megan felt she'd got into an operetta. She said so, inhaling the delicious fragrance of the flowers.

"Everyone puts on his best clothes to welcome the lady of the manor. We are still—feudal at Vellanti, Miss Royce." Cesare's voice was light; his eyes were cold.

"What's *that* supposed to mean?" Megan wondered angrily. But the car was emerging from the tree-lined avenue into a long approach drive, surrounding a green velvet lawn in the midst of which a fountain sent silver spray leaping upward, and Megan forgot everything else.

To the end of her life, she would remember the first sight of Vellanti. No modern landscape architect would ever equal the harmony of lawn, fountain, side plantings, curving drive . . . all leading the eye to a perfectly proportioned small castle of weathered white stone, with crenellated roof rails and chimneys upthrust at the corners. Megan's eyes filled with tears; it was so lovely, *so lovely*—and she was going to stay *there?*

Not, it developed, actually there . . .

Jumping out of the car and turning to assist his mother, Cesare eyed Megan with disfavor. "I regret, no rooms are prepared for Miss Royce, since we were unaware she was expected."

Amazingly, Ugo growled, "The Contessa will wish Mees to occupy the Blue Suite—I tell Maria; in only a few moments, all is ready."

"No. Miss Royce has been very ill; she's to rest, do nothing, for as long as I can keep her," Mrs. Waldron smiled mischievously over her shoulder at Megan. "Prepare Casa Piccola; Casa Grande will be far too *affairée* at the moment." Regally, she turned to the shallow marble steps—and the scene was straight out of Lehar, Friml, *Student Prince,* and *Blossomtime!*

Lining both sides of the steps were maids in bright-colored cotton skirts covered by intricately embroidered aprons. A row of footmen stood behind them in formal plum-colored uniforms embellished with rather a lot of gold braid. Fiercely mustached farm and garden workers stood humbly at the bottom by the shrubbery, wearing faded but immaculate smocks and twisting their caps in gnarled hands.

Megan thought, "Well! It certainly beats Radio City Music Hall!" Automatically, she programmed the scene: Entrance of Countess Giulia, accompanied by Cesare, Her Son. "Who am I?" Standing quietly beside Elise, observing Mrs. Waldron's handling of the starring role, Megan assigned herself the role of Ilse, Companion to Countess Giulia, and she held her face straight with an effort at this concept.

Strictly speaking, she ought to be a middle-aged shrew mouse of subnormal intellect, with a lisp . . . possibly a nervous giggle?

Meanwhile, Mrs. Waldron was ascending graciously, amid curtseys and bows, to a final flourish of hand kissing and a welcoming speech from the apotheosis of all *gros bonnets* . . . after which she swept grandly into the castle.

It was a perfect performance, but it was immediately ruined by a resounding inquiry. "Megan? Where *is* that girl?" Mrs. Waldron reappeared in the doorway. "What *are* you doing down there?"

"Admiring you."

Mrs. Waldron's lips twitched slightly. "You can do it better in the salon."

Megan trotted up the steps with a laugh. "I won't apologize for gawping like a rustic—because I am, when it comes to a place like this."

That was true, Megan thought later, but practically anyone would be overwhelmed by Vellanti. There was incredible luxury. What should be modern for comfort was the last word. The bathrooms looked like a Kohler ad; the décor of salons, study, and reception rooms rivaled a *Town and Country* spread on homes of Mrs. Guinness or the Duchess of Windsor —but there was a subtle difference.

One felt that Vellanti had always been here, merely growing like Topsy—that it owed nothing to an interior decorator. Fabrics and color schemes might be renewed, but the portraits hung today where they'd been placed, when delivered by Messrs. Titian, Fragonard, or Laszlo. One felt that a triptych commissioned in 1480 had been set on an inlaid table and never repositioned—merely accompanied later by a tiny Cellini cup and a Fabergé egg.

Yet even while Megan ate the delicious dinner from Meissen plates and sipped wine from Waterford crystal, she could agree that all, but *tutti*, was spoiled—by the sulky presence of Cesare. Now she was conscious of infinite weariness. "If only he'd *shut up*," she thought irritably, as he repeatedly addressed his mother in a spate of Italian and excluded Megan, until reminded, "Speak English, Cesare."

Then he'd throw himself back in his chair, lapsing into disgusted silence for a while, before trying again. It was a most uncomfortable evening, and at dinner's end, Cesare tossed aside his napkin and flung out of the room, after flatly refusing Mrs. Waldron's request that he escort Megan to the guest house. "Send one of the servants!" And of course that was a remark Megan understood, although in the face of her hostess's embarrassment, she pretended she hadn't.

Demitasse and liqueurs before a cheerful little fire was infinitely more pleasant without him, but Megan was now so indignant at his behavior to his mother's guest that she was determined to stay. "*J'y suis; j'y reste!* Sulky brat . . ." she thought.

"It is only nine o'clock," Mrs. Waldron was saying, "but I think we will call it a day, shall we?" She gave rapid instructions to a footman. Then, as Elise called, she said, "Yes, Elise, I am ready—goodnight, my dear. Ugo will be here shortly." She patted Megan's cheek gently and went away to the stairs.

Megan couldn't resist asking, "How's the ankle?"

Mrs. Waldron eyed her blandly. "A miraculous recovery! What do you think of that!"

"Not much," equally bland. "*I* suspect fraud."

"Shall we say—exaggeration? You were a good child; you do need rest; why not here—where I can amuse myself by clucking maternally?" With a final smile, Mrs. Waldron vanished, leaving Megan to finish her cigarette and stare drowsily at the fire . . .

"Mees? I regret so long a time you wait." Ugo's ugly unsmiling face loomed over her, lantern in hand.

"*N'importa.*" She struggled erect, sleepily realizing that her handbag was still in Mrs. Waldron's sitting room, where she'd combed her hair before dinner. Hesitantly, she said, "I've left my bag upstairs; has the Signora gone to bed, or would it be all right for me to run up and get it?"

"*Si,* I wait."

She was up the marble steps, moving along the hall, when she was aware of tempest: she heard Cesare's deep voice upraised, crashing noises, doors violently opened and shut . . . Mrs. Waldron's firm, "*Non parli stanotte, e abbastanza, Cesare! Andi, andi!*" Megan whirled to retreat, but with a final resounding crash, Cesare threw open the door and stood in the hall, thundering vehemently into the suite, while slightly muffled by distance was an equal torrent from Mrs. Waldron. "Wow, what a fight!"

Megan raced for the stairs, but before she could get down, Cesare's long strides had brought him up to her. His face was a devil mask, and involuntarily she shrank back against the marble balustrade, while he paused abruptly, eyeing her through slits that widened into flashing fury. She'd not the faintest idea what he said, but he spat it out like a cat, bending forward with hands curled into claws . . . until Megan felt reckless. She flung up her chin and glared at him. "*Stupido,*" she hissed, "*Domani, domani! Will* you get to hell out of it and leave her alone until tomorrow!"

"Hah! Miss Innocence, Miss Clever One!" he

sneered. "You do your work well, *biscia*—I hope you collect payment in advance, or that you never get, hah!" He straightened up with a contemptuous shrug and vanished along the opposite hall, with a final vicious slam, while Megan pulled herself together, Ugo was still waiting, impassive, not even raising his eyes from contemplation of the tesselated floor. Was he accustomed to such scenes? He must know what Cesare had said; "bitch" would be the least of it, she thought wearily. *Biscia*—wasn't that a snake?

Shakily, she went back to the upper hall, to the suite—might as well get the handbag since she was here. "*C'est moi, Elise . . .*"

"*Oui, ma'mselle . . .*" There was a flurry of unlocking and unbarring, and finally the maid's wary face peeked through the crack, relaxing at the sight of Megan. She handed out the purse and nodded tersely to Megan's apologies for disturbing Mrs. Waldron—but as she went away to the stairs, Megan heard the bolts again, and the key.

Why should Contessa Giulia Vellanti di Frecchia Waldron require bars on her private suite? Perhaps they had always been there, though—and how useful they must be, if these violent scenes were standard!

She went steadily down to the hall. "I'm ready . . ." Ugo picked up his lantern, swung open the door, lighted Megan efficiently down the entrance steps, and silently indicated a path to the right; Megan followed in silence; once she stumbled on an unsuspected step. Ugo's hard hand gripped her arm at once, but he said nothing beyond "Goodnight, Mees" when they reached the entrance to the guest house.

She felt rather than heard his departure, while she was still facing the great wrought-iron door. "*Wait,*" she gasped, faintly. Did he expect her to go alone into a totally strange house? On top of physical fatigue and the ugly scene she'd inadvertently witnessed, Megan's eyes filled with tears, both of fright and anger. For two cents she'd have sat on the top step and bawled. Definitely, she couldn't stay here, after all; she hadn't physical strength to combat Cesare and his henchmen.

Before her tear-blurred eyes, the door swung open slowly—and a pair of bright dark eyes peered at her. "Ah, I *thought* I heard someone—come in, come in, Signorina. I am Anna Maria, to wait on you."

A neophyte maid, Megan decided, as the girl bumbled about, willing but inexpert, giggling infectiously over her mistakes. She was all the disdained visitor might expect—yet in her own way Anna Maria was soothing, for she was proud to be chosen to wait on Mees and very anxious to please. "If I stay—*if*," Megan told herself grimly, "I'll *fix* that Cesare! I'll turn this girl into an expert. Hah, himself!"

She was a gone goose the instant she hit the bed; nothing had ever felt so good! She was scarcely aware of Anna Maria adjusting shades, turning off lights, departing with a bobbing curtsey, "*Buon' sonno*, Mees."

It was nearly ten before Megan awoke, to clear sunshine and the scent of roses. Anna Maria produced breakfast on a terrace table; smilingly she permitted Megan to practice basic Italian, interspersed with occasional giggles. Comfortably filled with omelet, hot buttered toast and lashings of coffee, Megan looked idly at the lake. "It is really I; I am really sitting on an Italian terrace, sniffing roses, looking at Lombardy poplars and Lago di Como!" Impossible

—yet it was true, and in daylight, life was once more unreal, to be anticipated.

She was considering, not very energetically, the concept of exchanging lounging robe for proper clothing, when a shadow lengthened on the tiles, and Cesare di Frecchia emerged from the salon door, Anna Maria bobbing and smiling behind him. All Megan's irritation returned. Who did he think he was, to be shown in without asking whether she wished to receive him? "The rudeness, the arrogance," she fumed inwardly; "I bet he still believes in Droit du Seigneur!"

She got a good long look at him, walking the length of the terrace, and he was still nothing to wave flags about. Oh, he was taller than the average concept of Italians—and undeniably he was graceful, which was fine if you liked panthers, but his nose was crooked . . . and by the expression on his face, he was all set to ruin Megan's one day at Vellanti. Because she'd already, regretfully, decided she mustn't add to Mrs. Waldron's problems by causing dissension.

"Good morning," he said formally. "I trust you slept well, Miss Royce?"

"Very well, thank you."

"I have come to apologize for my failure to make you welcome last night. I beg you to forgive my ungraciousness."

"You should rather apologize to your mother," Megan returned impersonally. "I am her guest, not yours."

Cesare stiffened, throwing out his chin as if she'd slapped him. "You do not accept my apology?"

"No," she said calmly, "because you are not really sorry to have embarrassed your mother, who is not a

47

young woman, who was physically exhausted by near-ly twenty-four hours of travel, including a painfully wrenched ankle . . . who was doubly humiliated be-cause she loves you and wished to be proud of you to a stranger." Cesare whitened and glared at her, but Megan gave him no chance to say a word. She was thoroughly infuriated, herself . . . and not merely for the lost chance to rest gratis in this beautiful place, but because she suddenly realized how dreadfully Mrs. Waldron was going to feel when Megan quietly packed and left.

"If you loved her, you'd have made last night a peaceful homecoming and allowed her time to rest before inundating her with whatever this is that's so important to you," she said bitingly. "But no! *You* destroy her pleasure, add to her weariness, by sulks and arrogance to her guest. If you knew how she looked forward to Vellanti, to repaying me for minor kindness . . . and if you knew what I went through at Orly, to make her comfortable . . . !" Megan snorted, scrambling to her feet. "No, Mr. di Frecchia, I *don't* accept your apology. I tell you again: apologize to your mother. Now, if you'll excuse me . . ."

"Wait!" he said, imperiously.

"What more's to be said?" She continued toward the door, but in two steps he'd caught her arm. "Please?" he asked, gently. "I am at fault, I confess it—but now let us understand each other?" He rum-pled his hair distractedly, while Megan hesitated. "Al-ready I have had such a scolding from Mama! She even said I was a disgrace to the name of *both* Vellanti and di Frecchia—and that is the ultimate. Mama never invokes that unless one is really bad! Please," his fingers tugged urgently, "you must help me redeem myself."

"He turns on charm like a water tap," Megan thought, half contemptuously—still, why not try for a modus vivendi, and perhaps she needn't distress Mrs. Waldron by rejecting the invitation. She allowed herself to be led back to the table where she accepted fresh coffee and a cigarette. "Well?"

Cesare tossed the cigarette lighter absently from hand to hand. "It is—a family matter," he began.

"With which I have nothing to do!"

"But I do not *know* this, and always I am impulsive." He smiled wryly. "Something my family never forgets, I assure you! 'Another of Cesare's mad schemes, that only cost . . .'

"It has been two *years* since Mama was here! I went to New York three weeks ago to beg, to implore her to visit, see for herself; she is receptive; I have every hope," he said, tight-lipped, "and she arrives—*with you*. Even, she says, you were hired by 'Renzo. What *can* I think, Miss Royce, when Mama hides behind you, saying, 'No, no, no—wait a while'?"

"You said you thought I was your brother's mistress," Megan observed, with detachment.

His eyebrows flew upward in incredulity. "*I* said that?"

"You did."

"Well—I confess I am impulsive," he said after a moment, stroking his chin and eyeing her critically. "Now that I look at you, Miss Royce, you are not at all 'Renzo's taste, which," as her eyes widened angrily, "is regrettably—*ordinary*! In fact, I should say you are much more my pigeon than his," he murmured, "so it is imperative we forgive each other, no?"

Megan sternly resisted the wicked twinkle in his dark eyes. He might be rather fun if he straightened out and flew right. "But *I* have done nothing requiring amnesty," she said sweetly, "and as to pigeons —I'm more used to eagles, Mr. di Frecchia."

"You were hired by my brother. . . ."

"Oh, for heaven's sake get off the G string," she said impatiently. "I was hired by telephone to sit beside your mother, see her onto the Milan plane—and *leave*. Yes, it's obvious there's some family problem; it has nothing to do with me, except," she sprang to her feet, "I'd appreciate your arranging for me to be driven to some inexpensive *penzione* nearby."

Cesare's face went blank at the repudiation of his invitation to a flirt. "You wish to depart?"

"No—and yes," Megan said, evenly. "I'd ask nothing more than to accept your mother's invitation to rest here for two weeks—I really have been ill—but not at the cost of her daily humiliation. I *like* your mother. Oh, don't worry," as he opened his mouth, "I'll be tactful. I wouldn't hurt her for the world . . . and if I weren't physically exhausted," she added deliberately, "I wouldn't leave. I'd stay right here, and *be* in the way, and the hell with whether you hate your brother! If he's anything like you, he deserves it."

Megan went steadily to open the terrace door, looking back at the tall, impassive figure. "How such a sweet person as your mother ever spawned anything like you, I'll never know," she told him clearly. "Have a car ready at five, please, and tell someone to arrange a room somewhere—anywhere!" While he stood immobile, she went across the little salon and up to her room, where she closed the door and went blindly to a window, stifling sobs.

Damn him, *damn him*—what was she to say to Mrs. Waldron? Leaning against the curtains, she could see Cesare striding away along a path to the left, swiftly lost behind shrubbery. Blotting away tears, Megan moved sadly from one window to another; *nothing* could be better than to stay here among all this beauty, but he'd make it insufferable. Already she was shaky from the interchange. "Be philosophical," she told herself firmly. "Already you've had more than you expected. Make the most of the one day at Vellanti, at least." Decisively, she turned to find slacks and walking shoes.

If only she had the faintest idea why everyone was so suspicious of her. First Mrs. Waldron, though once she'd known Megan had been hired by 'Renzo not Cesare, she'd been satisfied . . . But it was vice versa with Cesare: everything had been okay, *until* 'Renzo had cropped up. One shoe on, one shoe off, Megan considered, frowning. Everything pointed to Lorenzo as the favorite son—yet every instinct in Megan said Mrs. Waldron preferred Cesare! She'd no clear-cut idea of how she knew this, but know it she did—and she could feel the shakes returning inside her. No matter what excuse Megan made for leaving when she'd hardly arrived, Mrs. Waldron was going to be heartbroken that her beloved son should behave so impossibly—because she wouldn't be fooled for a minute! She'd know that Megan was going because she couldn't stand Cesare. Oh, *damn*!

From her bedroom windows, Megan carefully noted the path to Casa Grande, the path to the lake, a subsidiary path that seemed to end at a greenhouse. Other paths led upward behind the castle, across fields to woods at one side, to a row of beehives on the other side with a small vineyard, an orchard brave with blossoms, and thence over the hill—to a village. Megan could just see the tip of a church steeple.

Her heart yearned to Vellanti—there was so much

to explore, simply to contemplate, appreciate, at leisure. "I wouldn't be in anyone's way; I could stay down here, take little walks, and maybe say 'hello' to Mrs. Waldron when she wasn't too busy."

But it wasn't possible, and thank goodness Megan had enough money to be independent. Get it over with, she decided, as Anna Maria smilingly closed the iron-grilled door behind her. Megan took a deep breath, sauntered toward Casa Grande, considering what in hell to say. . . . She didn't want to reflect on people or things; could she possibly get away with claiming that the lake air proved bad for her chest? She could try it, anyway; no matter what she said, Mrs. Waldron would guess the truth.

Megan rounded the curve of the path, emerged from the clipped yews and the scent of roses rioting along the low marble balustrade marking the drive-way—and stopped short. Before the entrance steps of Casa Grande stood a dashing white Porsche. Ugo was opening the driver's door and *smiling*! A most elegant figure descended gracefully, stripping off driving gloves, clapping them against his palm while he bantered with Ugo.

He was slender and dark, and he stood like a bantam cock, making the most of his few inches. *He was the man Megan had bumped at Orly!*

CHAPTER FOUR

The gears of Megan's mind meshed with an almost audible click—and she was still only in low speed. The man was Lorenzo di Frecchia, of course, and his mother had seen him at Orly. Now, "Has he gone?" made sense—yet why should Mrs. Waldron be so frightened, so relieved to share her seat with a strange girl in preference to her son?

What was he doing here anyway, considering the fancy tale he'd given Megan?

His arrival settled one difficulty: Megan would insist upon departure to permit a family reunion. Unobtrusively, she retreated—and back into a motionless body. "So, the master arrives to see how much you have accomplished, Miss Royce?" Cesare inquired softly. His hand gripped her elbow, and he propelled her inexorably forward. "Let us set his mind at rest."

"Let me go," Megan hissed furiously, but it was too late. Ugo had seen them, and at a word, Lorenzo turned, his face breaking into a delighted smile.

"Cesare!" he shouted joyously, throwing wide his arms and bounding forward to meet them. "And Miss Royce! How are you? Cesare has been conducting you about? Ah, I'd hoped for that pleasure!"

"Why?" Megan inquired blankly. "Who are you?"

"Lorenzo di Frecchia . . . but of *course*! We met only by telephone." He pumped her hand up and down, eyeing her appreciatively—and little as Megan thought of Cesare, she thought even less of this one!

"How d'you do." She withdrew her hand, slid free of Cesare's grip while 'Renzo was clapping him heartily on the back, and moved on to the castle. "I had no idea you were expected," she said clearly. "In fact, I thought the whole point of my accompanying your mother was entirely because you would be unable to leave New York until Wednesday—which is today. You must have traveled with the speed of light."

"Not quite that," he said, with an ingratiating shrug. "I find I can rearrange my business; I fly direct to Rome, to Milano, to Frecchia for the car— and here I am!" He turned to Cesare with a happy smile, rambling after Megan. "It is a surprise for Mama!"

A surprise it would definitely be, but not, Megan thought expressionlessly, a happy one. Ugo had vanished into the entrance hall; the great doors stood open, and by the car, Lorenzo was still being a little ray of sunshine, while his brother stood uncompromisingly before him. Megan faded silently into the foyer, sped up to the master suite.

"*Elise, c'est moi, ouvre vite, vite!*" Hurrying into the sitting-room, Megan motioned for Elise to refasten the door. "Lorenzo is here!" The maid's face tightened instantly, and she slid the bolts and turned the huge key at once—not a moment too soon. Already, a knock came at the door, and a shouted "Mama?" There was a furious rattle of the door knob. "*Mama?*" Megan backed away shakily, but Elise was evidently experienced at handling Mrs. Waldron's sons. "*Qui est là?* Madame is resting."

"Well, rouse her, Elise! It is I, Lorenzo—and Cesare with me—we come to *déjeuner* with mama . . ."

"Rouse madame? You know better; *allez-vous-en!*" Elise leaned comfortably against the door while a major spluttering began in the hall. She replied in French invective that sent a barrage of Italian into orbit, which raised Elise's voice to ultra high frequency and very colloquial argot. Judging by the decibels, Lorenzo was once more jumping up and down as at Orly; every so often a deeper voice would attempt to say something, only to be shouted down by the falsetto. Nobody paid any attention to anyone else, and it was total impasse, because the door was securely barred, and Elise wasn't about to open it.

In a horrid way, the scene was hilarious. Megan was suppressing giggles—until the inner door opened and Mrs. Waldron stared at them, white-faced.

"*Tais-toi,*" Megan said to Elise, and she ran to catch the swaying figure. "Oh, we didn't mean to wake you . . ."

"That was 'Renzo's voice. What does *he* want?"

"To breakfast with you." Megan gently urged the older woman into the bedroom.

"*No!* Not both of them; I can't stand it . . ."

"Well, that is what Elise is telling them." Megan nudged the door closed with her foot, and saw at a glance that Mrs. Waldron had breakfasted; had been lying on a chaise longue by the window and examining some sort of business papers. Without comment, she resettled her hostess on the lounge, drifted the afghan over her toes, and found cigarettes and a lighter. "More coffee?"

"No. Sit down, Megan," Mrs. Waldron said abruptly. "You must wonder why I am barricaded against my sons."

"Not after this sample of Latin temperament! All the same, now you'll be wanting a family reunion, so I'll transfer to a *penzione*."

"No, *please* don't desert me! Let me explain . . ."

"Really, it's not necessary," Megan protested uncomfortably, but Mrs. Waldron was clutching her arm distractedly.

"At first, when I knew you were hired by 'Renzo, I thought . . . but at once I knew you were honest, Megan. The ankle was true; I made it seem worse because I saw it would help us both: you need rest and must save money—and I need time. I thought a stranger would curb Cesare," she sighed wearily, "and instead I've only exposed you to rudeness. Now, 'Renzo will make things twice as difficult."

She closed her eyes and sank back on the lounge, patting Megan's head lightly. "Oh, I'm a selfish old woman, my dear! Forgive me, I forget you have been ill. You must go to the Albergo Dante as my guest— no, I insist, Megan! I assure you," she snorted faintly, "your hotel bill will be *soldi* compared to what my sons want!

"I had so many plans. You're a most companionable young woman, and my daughter, Luisa, is a stupid cow," she said with sudden energy. "She looks at my mountains and says 'Very pretty'—and next moment asks if our milk is tuberculin-tested!"

"Oh, all right—never let it be said I deserted Mrs. Micawber!" Megan laughed helplessly. "I'll stay, but a bigger bunch of con artists I never met! Are you descended from Machiavelli, by any chance?"

"I believe so, or perhaps only the Medicis," Mrs.

Waldron said vaguely. "But much as I want you, I won't allow you to risk your health, Megan."

"I need physical rest, principally: no schedules, no fighting traffic night and morning—but my *mind* isn't tired, except of my own problems. It will be good for me to think of yours . . . but I'd better tell you," Megan said thoughtfully, "that I don't much like your sons. Cesare's a sulky brat, and Lorenzo's a liar."

"However did you grasp this so quickly?"

"Lorenzo told me he rearranged his business and flew direct to Rome—but he was the man whose seat I got at Orly. You saw him; you knew I saw him, too, and didn't recognize him; evidently he doesn't know he was seen—but why lie?"

"Because his plan failed." Mrs. Waldron considered silently for a moment. "You have to know some things, even if you prefer not. 'Renzo inherited Frecchia as older son; Cesare will have Vellanti when I die; Luisa is married to a rich American. The money is mine, mostly from Lucius; it will be split equally at my death. The business interests were set up by Uberto, to avoid Mussolini. After the war, 'Renzo chose to manage personally." Her lip curled slightly. "Meaning the staff does the work, while Prince Lorenzo di Frecchia makes the most of his title and money in New York gossip-column society," she continued. "I hear he can be persuaded to lease Frecchia to parvenus—at rather exorbitant sums."

Megan's eyes widened. Was Cesare a prince, too? He was! Mrs. Waldron went on: "Cesare is like his grandfather. He cares little for the title, everything for Vellanti—and has no head for business, poor boy. The money he's wasted, trying to restore the estate since the war! This latest plan seems more mature, as he explained it to me in New York. I agreed to see for my self." She snorted dryly. "Well—you've seen? How can one think?"

"He *is* a bit single-gauge . . . and 'Renzo wants to queer the deal?"

"*He* had a plan to expand the business."

"Hmmmm. Well, you think, and I'll be 'X.' Don't you see—each knows I'm not for him," Megan chuckled, "*but* am I committed to the opposition, or can I be lured to lend support? You'll see, they'll be smooth as whipped cream. What fun!"

"It's not a joke, Megan! I warn you, don't expect American rules—remember these are violent temperaments!"

"Oh, what can they do?" Megan countered sturdily. "Scream at me, is all—and they won't dare, for fear of upsetting you." She smiled at Mrs. Waldron's somber face. "Incidentally, what do I call you?" she asked. "'Mrs. Waldron' seems sort of out of place here. The servants all call you Contessa; Elise says Madame, and I suppose you're also a Principessa."

"What would you like to call me?" Mrs. Waldron asked with a smile. "And I may say I am opposed to 'courtesy' kinships."

"Oh, me, too!" Megan agreed feelingly. "My childhood was made hideous by trying to remember whether it was Cousin Polly and Aunt Florence, or vice versa." She considered briefly, eyeing her hostess. "I don't think we'd either of us be really happy if I tried to call you Giulia," she said, finally, "but I think we might get used to 'Tessa, as short for Contessa. How do you feel?"

"The perfect solution!" The dark eyes sparkled with kindly inscrutability. "It will be nice to have a friendly informal name between us, Megan. Yes, Elise?" she asked, as the maid whisked into the bedroom, looking smug as a cat.

"They have gone."

"You mean they have retired," Megan observed, "but I'm afraid they'll be back again." She stood up and grinned at Elise. "I'm on your side," she stated, reassuringly, "and if you'll lend your support, we'll be the most inconvenient women that ever frustrated two Italian juvenile delinquents *manqués*."

"*C'est vrai*," Elise agreed dramatically. "*Ah, les punaises* . . . to disturb Madame!"

Megan controlled her face with an effort. "As soon as they crawl out of the woodwork, we'll push them in again, Elise! 'Tessa—I'll leave you to yourself and see you at dinner."

Refreshed by three hours of siesta, Megan descended to the foyer of Casa Piccola, with Anna Maria in admiring attendance. The entrance doors stood open to the soft night air. A male figure lounged against the balustrade, but at the click of high heels, he straightened up and turned into Prince Cesare.

"*Buona sera*, Miss Royce. I came to walk up with you."

"How kind—I was quite satisfied with Ugo."

"Unfortunately, he is occupied. I fear you must accept a substitute."

"It's not really necessary," she said indifferently, while Anna Maria draped the evening shawl over her shoulders. "American girls are extremely good at figuring how to walk up a path without a map . . . particularly when dinner is at the end."

His lips twitched faintly. "Well, it is obviously a

wasted effort. However, I am here; I must also go there, in order to achieve my own dinner, and I confess a hearty appetite, Miss Royce." He led her to the porch, picked up an iron-bound lantern and debated absently, "Will you prefer to take this, while I follow at a discreet distance? I must warn you these lanterns are heavier than they look—and my legs are longer than yours, though not so well shaped—inevitably I shall overtake you"—he squinted reflectively—"just as you have found the upper bench . . . and it will manifestly be impossible for me to pass by with only a polite nod."

"Why not?"

"Abandon a lady alone on a marble bench?" he protested. "Impossible! Chivalry demands I sit beside you and describe the landmarks within sight—and we will both be late for dinner . . . something Mama detests."

"Oh, dear, I'm afraid I'm being very inconvenient."

He raised the lantern and surveyed her deliberately. "Yes, you are," he agreed after a moment, "but it does not follow that the inconvenience is unwelcome, Miss Royce. If you are ready?"

Silently, Megan laid her hand on his arm and descended the shallow steps. "One up for him," she recorded mentally, pacing along in the half-light, until suddenly the crenelated roof and upper lights of the castle glimmered above the yews. Involuntarily, she paused. "It's like a medieval painting!"

"I told you we are still a bit feudal at Vellanti."

"Yes—but I wonder why you think an American incapable of understanding loyalty, Prince Cesare."

The lantern swung uncontrollably in the convulsive tightening of his fingers. "I don't," he said, guiding her up two steps to the bench. "There is only the question of—to whom they give their loyalty."

"Traditionally, Americans seem to back only winners," she murmured, "although I suppose the winners are sometimes only victorious because of American backing. Ah"—she sank onto the bench—"you were right—the view is superb!"

Silently, Cesare set the lantern on a low pillar and offered a cigarette. "I'm happy you reversed your decision to leave, Miss Royce," he said suddenly, "but I confess amazement at the rapid alteration in your mind."

"Woman's privilege. . . . What are the tiny lights directly below?"

"Our boathouse—and that," he said, as a double tier of lights placidly rounded a tree-dark point, "is the last boat from Lecco." Megan bent forward, absorbed in the play of light and shadows, while he mused, "Women have so many privileges, have they not? Particularly when they are Americans and beautiful . . ."

From the corner of her eye, Megan could see fingers tensed to breaking point about a cigarette; could sense utter discouragement. Of course—he'd interpreted her words to mean she was on Lorenzo's team! Impatiently, she wondered why no one seemed to think the Contessa might have a team.

"The privilege in this instance belongs to your mother. She asked me to change my mind, and I agreed."

"That is—all the answer?"

"Enough, surely?"

Absently, he lit a cigarette, his eyes intent in the tiny flicker of the lighter. "You're very beautiful,

Miss Royce," he said suddenly—and the deep voice was surprised! "If only I knew where you stand . . ."

Megan gulped, completely caught off guard. "Squarely in the middle, buffer state, no-man's-land," she shrugged—and almost welcomed the rapid footsteps approaching above.

"Miss Royce! Cesare, why do you delay Miss Royce, when Mama is waiting!" Lorenzo's voice was nearly falsetto with anger. Looking up at him, bristling on the top of the steps and flourishing a lantern dramatically, Megan thought it amazing that dinner clothes emphasized aristocracy in one man and made the other a popinjay. No point to a scene à la Orly, though . . .

She rose apologetically and went up to tuck her hand confidingly into his arm. "I'm so sorry, but I had to rest for a moment . . . you remember, I've been ill? What sort of boats do you have? I'm a very good helmsman . . ."

It was the right red herring. Lorenzo immediately puffed away about the sailboat, power cruiser, runabout—interspersed with Yachtsmen I Have Known. Megan murmured admiringly, and occasionally she dropped a Name of her own. As they went up the castle steps, Lorenzo finished cordially, "All is at your command, Miss Royce."

"Not," said Cesare, "until she's demonstrated her competence to my satisfaction."

"Really, Cesare! You insult Miss Royce—anyone accustomed to the Sound, to Block Island, Newport . . ."

"Lake sailing is different, and," as Ugo swung back the great doors so that Megan stood spotlighted by the foyer lamps, "we must take no chances with any guest of Mama's—particularly one so young and beautiful, eh, 'Renzo?" Waving Megan forward politely, Cesare added, most distinctly and interpretably in Italian, "You certainly know how to pick 'em!"

Megan sternly suppressed a giggle, as she graciously dropped her shawl into Ugo's hands. If only he weren't such a self-centered oaf, Cesare might be fun. Ignoring the men, she moved serenely toward the small salon where the Contessa was ensconced *en grande tenue* of Paris gown with her a blaze of diamonds. "Good evening, 'Tessa."

The Contessa eyed her bland face impassively, until Megan could not repress a very vulgar wink. Lorenzo was bustling into the room, rubbing his hands together with satisfaction. "Here we are, here we are. We have brought Miss Royce."

"So I see. How charming you look, my dear. Come and sit beside me. We will allow the men to admire us together, shall we?"

That set the tone of the evening, and after a single very dry Martini (expertly mixed by Cesare) and two wafer-thin slices of very hot, very buttery toast, tenderly spread with fresh caviar (by Lorenzo), Megan felt alive for the first time in months—perhaps in all her life.

Here she sat: surrounded by wealth and aristocracy —and perfectly able to play it by ear, without embarrassment. "If Bob could see me now, hah!" she thought. Looking at the beautiful face of her hostess, Megan fancied it was already less strained. The conversation was principally in English, for Megan's sake—but even when the di Frecchias forgot and broke into Italian, the two men were a restraining influence on each other, keeping the subjects trivial and amusing.

Lorenzo unexpectedly emerged as an able raconteur with a wicked wit that brought tears of laughter to his family. Even while Megan laughed wholeheartedly, she could not suppress a faint suspicion that his scurrilous anecdotes were intended more to emphasize his high position and stability in international society than as good stories . . . but perhaps if she'd personally known the names he was dropping, she would not have had such an unworthy thought.

Certainly, 'Tessa and Cesare were enjoying 'Renzo's naughtiness to the full, chuckling and laughing heartily . . . occasionally inserting a comment that only drew a swift riposte from 'Renzo to send them into even heartier gales of laughter. Definitely, it was a brilliant evening, and one Megan knew she would treasure all her life.

It was wonderful to sit in the lovely room . . . to be leisured and comfortable, sipping her cocktail and nibbling caviar before a tiny fire . . . to be a part of the *haut monde en famille,* listening to the beautiful modulations of voice, the small literate allusions and the suave *mots justes* that were so cleverly and carefully chosen, yet tossed into the conversational pot as though of no value . . . It was all an enchantment, a major ego builder, to find herself able to follow the conversation with ease, even if she couldn't contribute to the bouncing ball of verbal thrust and parry; but in any case this was obviously 'Renzo's evening.

He stood short and dapper on the hearth rug, moving his hands dramatically, his eyebrows forming exclamation points. Megan looked at him thoughtfully, and he was still a bantam cock in her book; furthermore, one who was probably always "on" in order to compensate for those missing inches.

By contrast, Cesare was gawky but unexpectedly quiet, letting his brother hold the stage, lounging in a side chair with his long legs crossed, not missing a word but saying little . . . except, Megan noticed, whenever 'Renzo seemed about to run down, it was Cesare who offered the titbit to wind him up again.

And in the middle of dinner it was Cesare who nearly ruined everything by an impassioned description of the need for public housing in order to attract a better class of worker. The Contessa's face went blank and all the lines returned.

"Have you seen the reports of the New York Housing Authority, Prince Cesare?" Megan asked earnestly, and launched into a short authoritative lecture. "They have to check each home every month for damage— terribly expensive."

Cesare glared at her. "We are talking of Italy, Miss Royce—not the slums of New York."

"People are the same everywhere. No one values what he gets for nothing, and I shouldn't wonder if you'd have more trouble here," she reflected. "Peasants, you know. Even in New York slums, no one expects to keep pigs or chickens in the house, but here—" She shook her head. "Traditions are so hard to reeducate, don't you think?"

Lorenzo made the mistake of snickering, while Cesare sat taut-jawed, staring at his plate. "You put it excellently, Miss Royce! In a nutshell: Why invest in people and reap only ingratitude, when one can earn a handsome profit by lending money to aid exploration? Scant risk when one backs trained, experienced people—and where would the world be today if no one had ever sought for new minds, new oilfields?"

"Venture capital," Megan nodded comfortably, "but of course, not for oil in Italy."

"You sound very positive, Miss Royce," Cesare murmured.

"Oh, I am," Megan assured him, and presented a learned hash of the company files, liberally sprinkled with references to the Cretaceous sections and von Schnapp's analysis of the Eocene Age. Cesare listened with the deepest interest.

"So it would be useless to hope for oil at Vellanti?"

"Absolutely! There are no quinqueloculina in northern Italy, nothing but trilobites," she told him earnestly. "So you see? There would be no point to wasting money even for a seismograph survey! There may be some oil in Ethiopia—but you don't have that anymore, do you? Dr. Innisperg says . . ."

'Renzo found his voice finally. "*Who* is this Dr. Innisperg? By what right does he make statements . . ."

"Why, you know who he is," Megan said, surprised. "I told you the night you hired me, for heaven's sake. How can you run a business if you have that short a memory, Prince di Frecchia!"

Finishing her zabaglione, Megan noted that 'Tessa's face was calm once more—and gave Cesare a plus mark: he had not snickered at his brother's rout.

Lorenzo was summoned to the telephone; Cesare was needed in the estate office. Megan and her hostess sat cozily over coffee and liqueurs until nearly eleven. "I think I shall go to bed, my dear," said Mrs. Waldron. "One of the boys will be back shortly—or ring for a servant to light you down the path. Sleep well." The Contessa patted her shoulder lightly. "You are—invaluable!" she chuckled. "Bless you, bless you!"

"Goodnight, 'Tessa—tomorrow will be even better." Megan sat contentedly before the fire for a few minutes, then she roamed about the room, inspecting the bibelots carefully and enjoying them, until the ormolu clock softly tinkled twelve. She set down the Fabergé egg and went hesitantly to the foyer. It was darkened but for a night lamp at the bottom of the stairs. Her shawl lay on a side bench, but there was no one in sight, and no sound came from the servants' quarters. She swung open the great iron-grilled doors, half expecting to find Ugo waiting patiently with a lantern at his feet—but the steps were empty, and Vellanti was bathed in brightest moonlight.

Megan caught her breath at the enchanted silver beauty before her. It was midnight; why bother the servants? And, after her mischief during dinner, neither 'Renzo nor Cesare was likely to be a pleasant escort. . . . Megan slung the shawl about her shoulders and started for Casa Piccola, breathing deeply of the lake-damp night air, lingering to admire shapes and shadows of shrubbery. As the path began to slant more steeply, she slipped off her evening pumps and walked on the grass verge, until at last she stood just above the marble bench, and the balustrade of low pillars curved away to outline the drive, forcing her to cross back to the formal path.

For a full five minutes Megan leaned against the end pillar, simply looking: the lake, with a pinpoint of light here or there, moonlight in a silver streak spread across the water . . . behind her stood the castle, Casa Piccola; and far below was the dark blue of the boathouse.

She had a sense of contentment that was almost ecstasy. "It is really I, Megan Royce from Whitestone, New York—standing in the garden of an Italian castle . . . and the air is perfumed with roses. Gosh, everything they say about Italy is true!" Dreamily, she went across the path to bury her nose in the lush blossoms that were literally overburdening the bushes, so that half a dozen sprays drooped downward along the terrace. No one would miss a few flowers. . . . Delicately, Megan stepped from the embankment onto the marble bench, nipped off a generous handful of roses, and turned to step down to the path again.

As her eyes were on a level with the top of the path steps, which were flanked by the marble pillars and clear as new-shined silver in the moonlight, *she saw the deadly fine trip-wire . . .*

CHAPTER FIVE

Very carefully, Megan sat down and ferreted in her evening purse for cigarettes and match, looking anywhere but at the wire. The Contessa had warned her of "violent" temperaments; this would have been murder. If she had *not* removed the evening shoes, if she'd tittuped down the path, no matter how carefully—she would now be lying in a rag-doll heap at the bottom of the lower steps, having neatly fractured her skull against the top edge and slithered on through momentum.

"I wonder when I was supposed to be found? I do hope someone would have straightened my skirts," she thought, aware that she was in shock. It is no light matter to find that someone wishes to stamp "Paid" on your celestial account, after all—but gradually she emerged from shock to ratiocination. Whoever had set the wire had done so only *after* seeing Megan leave the castle alone. If she'd summoned a servant, there would have been no wire.

Would the trapper wait, to remove the wire instantly she fell? Was he watching her even now from the shrubbery shadows? If so, he couldn't be sure she'd seen the thing at all; her escape might seem pure chance. Megan lit a fresh cigarette and debated. More likely he'd retreat swiftly, to establish an alibi, and meant to return later. It would be safe enough to wait half an hour; no one but Megan would use the path at midnight.

What would be the most annoying retaliation? She decided to take the wire and go home and to bed. Megan arose, stretching casually, and wandered across to finish her cigarette, leaning against the pillar. The wire was so lightly twisted as to pull free easily, and in a twinkling she had it coiled into her evening bag.

Once in bed, with a sleepy Anna Maria yawning, *"Buon' sonno,* Mees," reaction set in. A length of ordinary picture wire—but why should either Cesare or Lorenzo be so afraid of her influence? She'd punctured their balloons equally at dinner, which certainly proved she had no axe to grind. The more she thought, the angrier she grew. What if she said to the Contessa, "One of your darlings tried to kill me last night, so I think I shall leave on the next carrier pigeon"? Hah, not a chance! If anything, it was flattery to be worth murdering. She fell asleep, clutching the wire and completely determined to give someone a nervous breakdown . . .

The casual way in which he emerged from a side path exactly as Megan left the guest house led her to suspect Prince Cesare had been lurking. In clear daylight, his saturnine face was unclouded. "Good morning, Miss Royce. If you can spare the time, I will introduce you to our boats."

It seemed impossible that this man had tried to kill her, yet why should it be Lorenzo? He smiled at her hesitation. "Mama is engaged with the overseers of the vineyards; there is plenty of time."

"I'm—distressed to inconvenience you."

"So you said last night," he said as he surveyed

her slender figure in slacks and sweater, "but even in daylight, I see no reason to alter my answer. You should wear green more often," he said impersonally, grasping her elbow and turning down the slope. "You have the eyes that color with the garment. Blue is good, violet would be better, but in green one also sees the chestnut tones in your hair. Now, we will see how much you know of boats. . . ."

It was a horrid, humiliating half hour, complicated by the appearance of Lorenzo just as Megan was struggling to memorize the unfamiliar foreign engine. "What are you about, Cesare! Anyone familiar with Newport is not to be put through tests. Move aside— I can explain to you in a moment, Miss Royce."

Between 'Renzo's inept and pompous instructions and Cesare's sardonic silence, Megan promptly forgot everything she'd begun to learn and could have cried with vexation. "I'd better study the engine at leisure," she said finally. "Could we try the sloop instead, if you've time to crew for me?"

"I am completely at your disposal, Miss Royce! Cesare, if you are busy, there is no need for us to interrupt you."

"Oh, I am equally free; just let me get the charts." He stepped easily to the dock walk, extended a strong hand to steady Megan, and went away to the map room while 'Renzo awkwardly scrambled from the runabout. Tenderly, he assisted Megan to the crosswalk for the next berth, where he made a show of jumping into the cockpit. "Tony Curtis you are *not*," Megan told herself, as the sloop quivered and yawed wildly. Ignoring his hand, she stepped down lightly and settled herself firmly at the wheel. Sailboats are the same everywhere, and looking at the sweet lines of the *Giulia*, Megan's confidence returned.

'Renzo perched beside her. "I cannot tell you how deeply glad I am that you are with us; Mama needs a young companion. She is not young; there are always exhausting—problems. I expect you know?"

"The trip was tiresome, of course"—Megan was deliberately obtuse—"but she looks forward to motoring and boating with me."

"Excellent! You have her confidence, in fact. An intelligent young American business woman can be of the greatest help to Mama." He laughed and patted her hand intimately. "Daily I am amazed at the good fortune! By your voice, I know you will please Mama; I confess I think wiser to engage you only to Orly— if there is any lack of rapport, she is not committed further. But if I'd had time to meet you, I should unhesitatingly have arranged exactly this: that you continue to Vellanti, to rest here as our guest."

"In a pig's eye," Megan thought vulgarly, hearing Cesare's footsteps. "I'm glad you're pleased with my handling of your commission," she shrugged with polite astonishment, "but you could scarcely have done more, in any case. It is your mother who owns Vellanti, and I am *her* guest." She withdrew her hand. "Shouldn't you be hoisting sail?"

"Of course, yes." 'Renzo was struggling with reef knots as Cesare dropped sailing charts into Megan's lap. "Perhaps you would care to study these?" he said, hard-eyed, and worked forward to unlock the water door and assist with the sails. Then he returned to cast off. Shortly they were into the lake and had caught a stiff little breeze—and Megan forgot rivalry, attempted murder, everything.

The *Giulia* was a joy, a darling, yard to an inch, and Megan nearly sang for sheer ecstasy. Ruthlessly she took the mainline from 'Renzo and applied herself to the tricks of the wind and the response of the boat. She was vaguely aware of Cesare handling the jib, but Lorenzo was still talking, dropping names, until Megan simply could not stand it!

"Coming about!" she called sweetly, and let the boom swing free. It caught 'Renzo neatly across the fanny, as he postured by the riding light, and swept him bodily into the lake. Automatically, Cesare sprang to toss a life preserver. "Ooops, I seem to have lost your brother. Can he swim?"

"He is an excellent swimmer."

Megan assessed the distance to shore as a quarter mile, and 'Renzo had the preserver. "Good," she said cordially, neatly adjusting the mainsail to scud forward. "Now you can stay the jib and direct me on the tricky bits."

"You did that on purpose!"

"Of course; he's no earthly use. Will you sit down, please. I should like to make a long tack toward that point."

"I do not understand you at all, Miss Royce."

"No, I thought you didn't. *Will* you sit down! I don't want to lose you, too; I can't handle her alone, and we're headed for a marker . . ."

Mechanically, he ducked to reverse sides, leaning to look back. "He's reached the ladder," he said. Megan said nothing. "He's likely to be extremely unpleasant about this, you know."

"You keep forgetting I *don't* know your brother— but after my incompetence in the launch, he was obviously taking his life in his hands when I was at this helm. I can only admire *your* courage, and now you may loose the jib line."

Cesare eyed her expressionlessly for a moment, until Megan dimpled at him innocently. "*Strega!*" he said, his shoulders shaking with silent laughter.

"Witch is preferable to snake—but neither is really accurate."

"Ah? How do you describe yourself, Miss Royce?"

"I told you last night: I'm no-man's-land." Megan tightened the mainline and adjusted the wheel slightly. "The jib, if you please . . ."

There was no sign of Lorenzo when at last they slid smoothly back into the Vellanti berth, tied sails, and locked the water door. "Could we finish the engine instructions?"

Cesare swung her up to the dock walk with a smile. "Why not? Let us put away the charts . . . see, they are stored here, when you want them." A half hour later, Megan had the guest keys. "Please don't try to handle the sloop or the power launch by yourself—and please never use the runabout without telling Ugo or Anna Maria or *someone*?"

"Yes, of course," Megan agreed absently. Looking about for the first time, as she followed Cesare up the steps, she was suddenly conscious of lapping water beyond the inner wall. "What's in there?"

"A berth for visiting boats, extra dinghies, canoes, what have you," he shrugged, throwing open the top door and standing aside while Megan stepped into a sort of pavilion, extending completely over the boat berths. This section was an immense recreation room, complete with fireplace, kitchenette and bar, dressing rooms and baths, game tables, and lounge chairs. Wow, what a place for parties!

Cesare was opening a lock, sliding aside panels in the window wall. Beyond was a wooden deck, half covered by a slat roof through which sunlight filtered down over hanging baskets of flowers and vines. "This is Mama's favorite spot. She does not swim well, but she loves to look at the water."

Megan went forward eagerly to the outer section, which was open to the sun and protected by a sturdy railing with flowers pots on each post. "What a beautiful view; no wonder your mother loves it."

"It is nicest from Mama's special chair." Cesare nodded to the rear of the shaded section, where a luxurious chaise longue was invitingly flanked by small tables and protected by an umbrella lushly flowered with improbable roses and Wisteria. Megan perched at the bottom as Cesare bent over the back to point over her shoulder. "From here one sees nearly to Menaggio and Frecchia itself . . . that is Isola ahead, Tremezzo beyond—Lezzeno across. The Bellagio point must be imagined, but one knows it is there by the boats coming around. Mama can sit here for hours, I assure you. I hope you like sunbathing?"

"Very much."

Cesare came forward, eyeing her wickedly. "The deck is screened for nudity," he remarked blandly, "to which Mama has no objection, but if you should be alone—adjust the inner blinds and present the 'Do Not Disturb' sign."

Megan could feel herself blushing under his teasing grin. She got up and followed him with a laugh. "Where do you keep the suntan oil?"

"In the dressing rooms . . . and this door leads to the path. You see—one goes either up to the veranda —or down and directly to the boats . . . and this is Mama's golf cart." He laughed softly. "I warn you, she goes everywhere—principally off the paths. For self-preservation, do you know how to operate these things?"

"Oh, yes." Megan slid in and started the motor. "As soon as *Tessa* has time, we plan to go boating and driving. Get in, please, and show me the correct paths?"

"Straight ahead, right at the intersection, and left at the main drive," he said after a moment, stepping in beside her. He sat silent until she'd turned onto the graveled road. "Where will these motor trips lead you?"

"I've no idea. Your mother wants to show me various scenic spots."

"No need for you to play chauffeur; Ugo or I will drive you wherever Mama desires."

Megan neatly braked the cart. "That isn't what we have in mind," she said politely. "We'd rather be alone . . ."

"So no one hears the conversations, so you may carry out your instructions?" Cesare's lip twisted. "Very clever, to knock 'Renzo overboard—where he could swim easily to shore—but already all was agreed between you, no?"

"*No* is right." Megan slid from the cart and lost her temper. "If you could see your ugly face right this minute, you'd realize no one would want *you* on a pleasure trip! You and your idiot brother—I'm *fed up* with the pair of you. I don't wonder your mother prefers a middle-class American secretary for company. I like her, not her money!"

Whirling on her heel, Megan ran up the steps, ignoring his urgent "Wait—you do not understand . . ." She was half tempted to say, "Don't I? I've a length of wire that says I understand too damn well!" But there would be no point to tipping her hand . . . Megan went quietly up to tap at the suite. "*C'est moi, Elise* . . ."

"Megan?" The warm voice welcomed her from the farther balcony. "Ah, you look stronger every day, *buono*! Sit down, my dear, and tell me how you have amused yourself this morning."

"Well, now I come to think of it, it was amusing, though perhaps you won't agree," Megan reflected. "So far I have knocked your son Lorenzo into the lake from the sailboat—and I pinned back *both* ears of your son Cesare in the driveway just now." She grinned mischievously at her hostess's blank face. "Anyone else you'd like me to tackle, 'Tessa?"

Oddly, things went much better for some time. 'Renzo went to Frecchia on business. His place at the dinner table was filled by Cardinal di Frecchia, a most imposing old man who was 'Renzo's godfather, but, as he seemed principally interested in gentle reminiscence with his sister-in-law, Megan ignored Cesare's sardonic silence. It was hard to believe that a Cardinal could be persuaded to exert deliberate influence for his godson against his other nephew; by evening's end, she realized the subtlety. Giulia was sincerely pleased to see Massimo, to forget the present in favor of old happy memories, overjoyed to learn that the Cardinal could spare a whole week to visit. Whether or not he knew what 'Renzo was up to, his mere presence would effectively distract Mama from her business decisions.

"Mean little skunk," Megan thought indignantly. "A good thing I didn't meet him first; I'd probably have refused the job!" She was half tempted to nudge the Contessa, but ethics prevented. She was buffer state, no-man's-land, on 'Tessa's team to protect her from undue influence. She couldn't express any personal opinion and ought not even to have one, but it was becoming difficult to remain unbiased. In Lorenzo's absence, Cesare was apparently catching up on his own affairs; he was in evidence only at dinner. Tactfully, Megan left 'Tessa to enjoy the Cardinal's visit, merely presenting her compliments each day, via Elise and the estate phone . . . after which she explored Vellanti.

One thing stood out: with the single exception of Ugo, who was polite but still dour, all the workers were obviously happy. They smiled; they worked hard and with pride; they loved the Contessa, admired Cesare, and welcomed Megan heartily. Wherever she went, she was warmly greeted; if she sat down for a minute, someone was sure to inquire solicitously for her health or offer a glass of water. In only a few days, her command of Italian had increased, she'd been cordially invited into most of the village homes, and her mind was a kaleidoscope of impressions.

She sorted them out on the lake in the runabout, alone—and ended in a state of impatience with Cesare for rushing his fences. If only he'd made a good show the first evening, he'd probably have had the money by now. Instead, he'd played directly into 'Renzo's hands, and it was going to be hard to reverse the bad impression.

To the ultimate question, Who tried to kill me? Megan had no definitive answer, although from dinner conversation she now knew Cesare was an expert picture restorer, had a studio fitted up in the other wing of the castle, even worked on paintings for family friends, and was highly respected by the Uffizi. There was no doubt that he had the most to gain, yet somehow he didn't fit. Why not? The best Megan could come up with: if he wanted to kill anyone, he'd do it in public . . . but in a way that was an answer. Cesare's violence was a matter of instant action, without plan or calculation. It was easier to imagine 'Renzo sneaking about in the shadows, but still not a *good* fit.

Again, why not? From the villagers, she knew that despite his pomposity, Prince di Frecchia had been active in the Underground. Once or twice she caught a naughty twinkle at the mention of *"il piccolo,"* but it was kindly. Vellanti honored Prince di Frecchia, and was unfailingly polite even if amused by his absurdities. There was a tacit "Let him throw his weight around, it does no harm . . ."

If 'Renzo wanted to kill her, he was capable of planning behind a smile—but instinctively Megan felt he'd think it beneath his consequence to execute the plan.

Which supposed a minion willing to murder on command? Oh, nonsense!

Once, she considered whether the trap might have been set by one brother to catch the other as he accompanied Megan, but it was unlikely that two people would hit the wire simultaneously for a dual tragedy. A final possibility: Was the wire meant for someone else entirely? The trapper had thought, by the lowered lights and silence in the salon, that Megan had long since gone . . . no, that wouldn't work, either; her evening shawl was in plain view on the hall bench—and who else could be expected on that path at such an hour?

For days Megan tried to put it out of her mind, only to squirrel back to the problem. It was useless to tell herself, "Forget it, you're alive." She was still furious, and she felt a tingle of regret. Almost, she felt apologetic to have caused anyone to wish to kill her. *"If I were Catholic, I could ask Cardinal di Frecchia . . ."* Yet, what to say? Not confession, really; Megan hadn't done anything. Still, the more she thought of it, the better it seemed. Suppose she asked for a few minutes alone with him—a priest was like a doctor; he couldn't reveal anything he was told . . . or was that only for communicants? On the other hand, how would it help to tell him—aside from merely unburdening herself?

The decision was made for her: an urgent message from the Vatican shortened His Eminence's visit by two days. Alerted by Elise, Megan walked up to the castle, and once more it was a scene—not operetta but grand opera—almost a medieval Passion Play . . .

Every possible servant, worker, worker's family, and all the babies and children for miles around waited quietly, reverently, for the Cardinal's blessing. Megan slid unobtrusively through the shrubbery to one side, while an apparently endless series of groups came forward to kneel on the steps before the magnificent red-robed figure.

Feudal, perhaps—but only fools and Communists disparage an occasional reminder that humans live more by faith than by animal instincts. Even Ugo stepped away from the waiting limousine to kneel among the house servants. Finally, there were only the Contessa and Prince Cesare, standing on the steps, with Megan politely to one side, lowering her eyes as they bent individually, first for a blessing, then for a parting family embrace.

"Miss Royce." The Cardinal smiled at her, extending his hand. "It was a great pleasure to meet you." His kindly face was suddenly serious and keen-eyed. "I sincerely hope to see you again and in perfect health."

"Thank you, Your Eminence," Megan said, and

looked at him earnestly. "Is there some sort of tiny blessing for outsiders?"

The Cardinal's lips twitched faintly, and for a second he was an old version of Cesare. "There is only one size in blessing, Miss Royce, and they are free for everyone." Silently, Megan bent before him, feeling a hand laid gently on her head and hearing the murmured words, and amazingly, it did feel infinitely peaceful and strengthening.

A bit awkwardly, she kissed his hand as the servants had done, and stood up—to be heartily enfolded by His Eminence in the family embrace. "I have a special blessing for you, Miss Royce," he murmured quietly, "for all you do for Giulia. I think you are what has been needed at Vellanti for many years. God be with you, my child."

He'd turned and descended the steps with 'Tessa and Cesare behind him, before Megan could say a word. In silence, she watched the final partings and his last gentle embrace for his sister-in-law. Then Ugo assisted him into the car, closed the door, and stepped away, as the Cardinal's chauffeur sent the car rolling forward, picking up speed until hidden by the trees.

"Megan." The Contessa's voice was gay. "You have stolen a march on me; you've been sunbathing! But this afternoon I will join you. Look at her lovely tan!"

"Most becoming," Cesare agreed, smiling, "but not entirely from the boathouse, Mama. Miss Royce has been everywhere; she is the friend of all Vellanti, I assure you!"

They were still under the spell of loving peace left by Cardinal di Frecchia; there were no undercurrents. "If you want to know anything, just ask me,"

Megan said proudly. "I am the original nosey-poke. I expect I ought to apologize for the lecture I read you about peasant housing, Prince Cesare." She laughed at his mocking grin as he assisted the Contessa up the steps, where Ugo now stood impassively by the great doors. "Oh, all right—I made most of it up, but you really were odious, and do you admit I played no favorites?"

"Yes," he said, but his dark eyes were thoughtful.

"I shall rest for a while," the Contessa announced, not attending to their conversation. "It was pleasant to see Massimo, but now we must return to normal. Ugo, I will lunch on the balcony and go down to the boathouse around two . . . will you come with me, Megan?"

"I promised to visit Maria to see the new baby, but I'll be back by three . . ."

Megan did not go to the village after all. Anna Maria was still uplifted while she served lunch, enumerating all the people who'd come for the Cardinal's blessing, but apparently she felt that this was an exclusive affair. She was definitely disapproving that various outlanders, including Maria's parents, had attended. "They're *not* from Vellanti . . ."

"I'm not, either, but His Eminence blessed me. He said blessings are for everyone."

Anna Maria was volubly unconvinced . . . but as Megan finished her ice tea, she decided to defer Maria. Her Italian wasn't good enough yet to cope with a clutch of relatives cooing over a new baby.

Accordingly, she changed to bikini, slacks, and shirt; rambled down to the boathouse; and opened the runabout berth. Swinging back the lake doors, she had an impression of sound above her. It was only one thirty, too soon for 'Tessa—the noise was probably made by one of the hanging baskets creaking in the wind. She climbed into the boat, gaffed carefully into the main stream, and drifted for a few minutes, studying the charts. Finally, she started the engine and headed toward Como at half speed, in order to explore the shoreline.

By now, Megan was known and recognized by the postman and by the captains of the lake steamers and the various delivery and vending boats plying back and forth regularly. She waved happily to everyone; not that she knew their names, but they were all friendly. At Cernobbia, she turned back to join 'Tessa by three . . . but thinking of her hostess, Megan was once more hatefully reminded of Vellanti problems.

She remembered the sweet face of Cardinal di Frecchia and his special blessing. Thank goodness she hadn't told him of the trip-wire! He might be unexpectedly keen-eyed and shrewd, but he was still an old man . . . To learn of attempted murder by someone in his family . . .

"Stop ducking the issue," Megan thought. "In your heart you know it was Cesare, but you don't want to admit it, because you applaud what he's done at Vellanti and admire the fierce devotion of the workers . . . He won't try again."

Why not?

Berthing the runabout, locking the water doors and going up to the veranda, Megan quoted Dr. Innisperg: "Extend the conclusions."

"Cesare acted hot-headedly," she thought. "It was my fault for infuriating him at dinner that night. He tried and failed; he knows I know it was tried—but by now, he also knows I'm not influencing 'Tessa. I haven't seen her alone for days; I haven't said a word at dinner that could be misconstrued. He knows I've been all over the place and everyone likes me . . . He even heard me offer to tell his mother what I'd seen; *that* goes to show I'm honest!"

Sliding open the glass doors, she found the veranda deserted but for the Contessa's lounge. It was nearly half past three; what had delayed 'Tessa? Megan yanked a pad from the pile and tossed it into a sunny spot near the chair and slid out of her slacks and shirt, but her mind was still troubled. Unconsciously, her eyes followed the afternoon boat from Como, which was disappearing about the Bellagio point, and she had a confused sense of infinite sadness.

Almost, Megan could have wept—that a man she could honestly have admired should be so flawed by stupidity, poor judgment, and suspicion; that he should act first and think later; that he couldn't see the woods for the trees . . . Why hadn't Cesare encouraged her to investigate immediately? Because he hadn't enough confidence in himself to dare the gamble! Megan's lip curled contemptuously; there was not a pin to choose between the brothers! If Lorenzo had sent his god-father to prevent decisions, it was going to prove a bigger mistake than hiring Megan—because it was only to be tactfully absent that Megan had, for the first time, wandered at will and slowly begun to form an opinion.

"You're not meant to take sides," she reminded herself. "You mustn't offer a word, mustn't even be enthusiastic if asked for a report. Remember, you're buffer state, no-man's-land!" Megan sighed and changed her mental subject. She must relax until 'Tessa arrived and think about the view and what sort of flowers are in the hanging baskets. . . . She leaned over, took a cigarette from the small table, flicked the lighter, and threw herself into the Contessa's lounge. With nightmare slow motion, accompanied by a hideous cracking noise, she felt the heavy frame sinking back, back and down, carrying Megan inexorably with it . . .

CHAPTER SIX

She wasted no breath in screaming; everything was reflex action. Tilting down into blackness, Megan rolled sideways and hit the icy water a split second before the chaise longue created a minor tidal wave. She came up shivering and spluttering, to find that the wrought-iron framework had vanished, leaving the long cushion floating disconsolately behind—but it was only waterproof, not a life preserver, she discovered when she attempted to pull herself out of the water for a breathing spell. Beneath any pressure, the cushion waterlogged and immediately gave up the ghost.

Frantically, Megan flailed at the water to keep warm by action. She was in the empty, blocked-off visitor's berth, with the lake doors closed and in total blackness but for the faint light through the gaping hole above her, where a dozen planks yawned downward with ugly spike nails wrenched lose from the veranda . . .

She felt her way completely around the berth; there were no steps, only bulkheads supporting the landing walk that was a full twelve inches beyond her reach. Nowhere could she find so much as a handhold on which to rest for a minute. She swam around twice, and finally connected—painfully—with the top of the sunken metal lounge frame.

It was apparently wedged upright, and unquestionably Megan's ankle was bleeding from contact—but at least she could rest for a moment and collect her thoughts, of which the first was, "Thank heavens, 'Tessa was late!"

The second was, "How in hell do I get out of here?" Even perched on the metal frame, she couldn't reach the landing, and already her body was numbing from the cold water. She would have to do something, or she'd lose her equilibrium and drown. She saw only one possibility: the lake doors. Megan swam over to feel down with her toes, and the bottom of the doors was about two feet below water! She took a deep breath, plunged, and in a few seconds was swimming vigorously to the outside ladder.

Averting her eyes from the hideous hole, she ran across to the dressing room, toweled briskly, and slid into a robe. Finally, she went back to inspect the damage. It seemed clear enough: a full yard of planking had loosened at the inner edge, and the weight of Megan's body added to the heavy chaise longue had done the rest . . . forcing the boards down until they cracked at the outer jointing.

They must have been hanging by a hair, ready to go at any moment . . . It was strange that they hadn't given way when Cesare stood behind the lounge to point out the landmarks—but if the wood had rotted in the two years since 'Tessa had visited Vellanti, perhaps it had only slowly released the nails, until today was the final touch.

Cautiously, Megan crept forward, plank by plank, alert for any ominous creak, but she reached the very edge of the hole without incident. Admittedly, she knew nothing of wood, but the broken ends looked healthy. Still cautious, she retreated and stood up. While she dragged another chaise longue from the games room and wedged it crosswise to block off the corner, the full horror hit her.

Sheer luck the Contessa had not arrived at two, when Megan was on the lake. Plunged into the yacht berth, she'd probably have drowned by now! "Mama does not swim very well, but she loves to look at the water . . ." How long could a woman of nearly seventy, who was not a strong swimmer, have survived the icy water with nothing to grasp and weighted by sodden clothes? Megan shivered uncontrollably, as the ship's clock in the game room sounded eight bells.

Four o'clock? Even if Megan had been on time (which she wasn't), it was highly doubtful she'd have been in time to save the Contessa. Even if she had been present to see 'Tessa disappearing through the rotten flooring, at hand to race down to the rescue, it would have been a devastating shock for the older woman.

To tell or not to tell? "I'll play it down," Megan decided. "I'll make a joke of it; I won't even say I fell in . . . just that I pushed the lounge while reaching for a cigarette, and it vanished into the briny deep."

She couldn't get away with it. The golf cart had arrived outside, and the Contessa and Elise were staring at Megan's wet hair and terry robe. "My dear child, something has happened?"

"Nothing, really! I was helping myself to one of your cigarettes, 'Tessa, and I stepped on some rotten planking"—Megan shrugged and smiled lightly—"and whoop-de-doo! I ended in the drink." She made a face of distressed apology. "Afraid I took your favorite chair along with me, I'm so sorry."

"Good heavens, don't worry about a chair—are you

all right, Megan?" The Contessa hurried forward—
and simultaneously, Cesare was standing halfway up
the inner staircase, his face ghastly white staring up
at her.

"Oh, I'm perfectly all right. I'm the cat with nine
lives, I am," Megan said deliberately. "You can't kill
me!"

Cesare came out of his suspended animation and
strode upward, two steps at a time. "How did you
get out?" he asked harshly, gripping her shoulders.

"Ducked under the lake doors," she said in a
"Doesn't everybody?" tone of voice.

"You might have drowned," he muttered, while the
Contessa and Elise were surveying the hole on the
veranda.

"Not *me*! But I do think it odd there's no ladder
in that one berth, Prince Cesare . . ."

He glared at her, half pushed her away from him,
and strode out to pull his mother away from the
scene of the crime . . . for that was quite definitely
what it was, Megan realized sickly.

"Those planks were deliberately loosened in order
to kill the Contessa," she thought.

"*Olà* Mama, where are you? Ah Miss Royce . . ."
Lorenzo trotted up the outer steps, to stop short
with a dramatic change of expression. "Something
has happened; there has been an accident? *Where is
Mama?*"

"On the veranda," Megan told him calmly, but as
he rushed past her, Megan's mind was suddenly
clicking. Who had alerted Prince di Frecchia for
this fortuitous arrival, the instant his godfather departed unexpectedly? Precisely when had he arrived
—*before* one thirty? Because now Megan was certain

89

that the noise she'd thought was creaking flower baskets was actually Exit of a Murderer, going quietly by the upper door, and unaware of Megan already behind the lower door, drifting in the run-about . . .

What would have happened if Megan had investigated that noise? With no reason for concealment, she'd have stepped forth to recognize the killer—and would instantly have been killed for her curiosity and her ability to say, later, who he was. Standing in the shade of the game room doors, she wondered impersonally how she'd have been dispatched. A bop on the head, perhaps—carted downstairs and tossed into the lower berth, to be joined later by the Contessa? Two drowned bodies—and Megan's blow ascribed to hitting the metal chair frame in an ill-fated attempt to rescue her hostess. *Ah, quelle horreur!*

Cesare had righted the chair Megan had used to block the corner, settled his mother comfortably, and was methodically moving about the hole. Lorenzo was rushing about, jumping up and down on various sections of the planking, and intermittently making furious comments in condemnation of his brother's criminal negligence.

"Methinks thou doth protest too much," said Megan's mind . . . for why should Prince di Frecchia instantly assume tragedy upon seeing, in a boathouse, a young woman who had obviously been swimming? Earlier in the season than most people might care to bathe, perhaps, but for all 'Renzo knew, Megan was a year-round Brownie. The conclusion was inescapable that he'd *expected* a fatality . . .

It was inescapable, too, that Cesare had been shocked, rocked on his heels, to learn that Megan had sprung the trap set for Mama. He'd given himself away by asking "How did you get out?"—so he'd known that it was a watery oubliette.

Thoughtfully, Megan looked at the brothers. Which? Or were they in it together? Were they trading information, realizing Megan was in the way for both of them? And when the trip-wire failed and there was still no definite decision by Mama, had they somehow tacitly agreed to get rid of *her*? Each stood to gain everything he wanted, merely by the death of the beautiful woman lying on the deck chair. Megan was suddenly aware of 'Tessa's strained white face, as Lorenzo held her hand, chattering excitedly, practically weeping at what *might* have happened. A tide of good Yankee piss and vinegar swept over Megan, sending her forward to stare down at the man, with surprised eyebrows and casual voice to counteract the bathos.

"Really, Prince di Frecchia, you're being extraordinarily tactless! Do stop harping on what might have happened, as though it were your mother's fault!" 'Renzo drew back, temporarily disconcerted, while Megan scooped up her slacks and shirt from the sun pad. "'Tessa, it's too late for much sun; let's leave them to repairs. Come back with me? Anna Maria will make us some tea."

"An excellent suggestion!" 'Renzo's face brightened; he sprang up, rubbing his hands delightedly. "Cesare, see to it while I take Mama to Casa Piccola."

"The cart only holds two people; shall I walk?" Megan asked, and let it lie there.

"Of course not; you come with me. 'Renzo, what are you thinking of? It is no party, after all." The Contessa's dark eyes flashed inscrutably, and she got up. "Elise, you will not object to following on foot?"

"*Mais, pas du tout.*" By the eager assurance, Megan knew Elise asked nothing better than freedom to inspect, wring her hands, and indulge in dramatics. *Ah, quel désastre!*

Stepping into the dressing room to collect her wet bikini, Megan thought, *Bien!* Elise would be most beautifully in the way of any consultations over the fiasco, any decision on a new plan. Did 'Tessa realize? Of course! 'Renzo's mawkish sentimentality had emphasized the reality. Clever 'Renzo, to turn failure into partial success, by pointing up the frightening ramifications! Megan set her jaw grimly. She could think later; there wouldn't be another attempt immediately; she'd have time to plan. All she knew at the moment was, "I'll see 'em in hell first!"

Swinging open the dressing-room door, she faced Cesare. "As manager of Vellanti, I must apologize, express my deepest regrets, for the uncomfortable experience, Miss Royce."

"Oh, think nothing of it, Prince Cesare," she said blithely. "No harm done after all, and it won't happen again."

"As always, you sound so positive, Miss Royce."

"Of course. There are never two fortunate coincidences, you know." She made to move past, but his hand caught her.

"What do you mean?" he demanded harshly.

"Why, you'll double-check *everything* from now on," she said. She smiled placidly and pulled away to go down the steps and slide into the golf cart next the Contessa. She felt rather pleased; *that* was the sort of ambiguous statement that should unnerve the lads . . .

At dinner, it backfired. "Miss Royce, I should appreciate it if you would not use the runabout tomorrow," Cesare stated. "I have given orders for Ugo to check the engine."

"Very well," she agreed, "I'll take your mother for a drive." -

"Not that, either, I'm afraid. I've instructed Ugo to dismantle the motors for a thorough overhaul; he won't be able to finish them for a day or so."

"Really, Cesare, how absurd! Why put everything out of commission at the same time?" the Contessa objected, but Cesare only smiled apologetically.

"It was Miss Royce's idea, Mama. After her disagreeable accident, she felt everything should be double-checked—and I must say, it seemed a sensible suggestion."

"What about the estate car?"

"It shall be immobilized also, but I've no objection to walking for a day or so." Cesare eyed Megan blandly. "A pity to confine you both, but better safe than sorry, eh?"

"Absolutely! The real pity is that you didn't think of this before your mother arrived, so all would have been in readiness for her." Megan was equally bland. "Never mind, 'Tessa. We'll think of something to amuse us; I have an inventive mind."

"You do, indeed, Miss Royce," Cesare murmured.

"All is not lost," 'Renzo announced. "You forget, there is my car. I will be happy to take you where you wish, Mama."

"*Grazie, caro,* but it would be uncomfortably crowded for Megan. We shall wait until Ugo finishes —and I have an inventive mind, also," the Contessa remarked. "Now is the moment for us to collect Elena's recipes for you, Megan—and I really should inspect the housekeeping, if only to gladden all hearts by enthusiastic approval. Come with me tomorrow, Megan, and we will poke about in the corners?"

"Delightful! Nothing I like better than poking into other people's corners . . ."

"I'm sure Ugo and Teresa keep Vellanti *immaculate*," 'Renzo said stiffly.

"Oh, I'm persuaded of it, and I'm not interested in dust," Megan answered. "I'm hoping for a ghost, holding its head under its elbow or clanking chains and groaning in the key of C minor."

"Improbable during daylight," Cesare observed, "but I believe, if Mama takes you to the other wing, you might find some bones in one of the closets."

"*Dry* bones?"

"Conneckit to de hip bone," he assured her, while 'Renzo huffed angrily, "What nonsense you talk; there are no ghosts or bones at Vellanti! Why do you frighten Miss Royce?"

Cesare raised his eyebrows. "I cannot believe anything frightens Miss Royce; you forget she is American, 'Renzo," he returned austerely; but at the wicked twinkle in his eye, Megan nearly choked for laughter.

"And you know very well there is a ghost at Vellanti, 'Renzo," the Contessa added, tossing aside her napkin and rising. "He's a Roman centurion, we think, and he's only seen near the upper springs—not at all frightening, Megan." She led the way to the salon, speaking over her shoulder. "And he may have gone away, because no one has seen him since about 1890."

"What a shame!"

"Depends upon the point of view," Cesare inserted. "*He* may be enormously grateful not to have to hang

94

about anymore—it's extremely damp at the springs . . ."

For the first time since Megan's arrival, a light rain began after dinner. "It will continue tomorrow, until the wind shifts," Cesare stated, producing a light coat and umbrella for Megan, "so you could not have enjoyed a drive in any case."

"But rain will not prevent Ugo from checking all the engines, so we may hope for fair weather and security on the following day," Megan agreed, serenely. "Isn't it amazing how often one has only to accept a temporary setback, only to find that all is for the best in the best of all possible worlds?"

"You put it well, Miss Royce," he said after a moment. "I am only sorry to have created the temporary setback to your plans."

"Oh, *I* have no plans, other than to be a companion to your mother when she wishes. If you are ready . . . ?"

Silently he picked up the lantern and opened the door. "Here, give me the umbrella, Cesare," 'Renzo called, trotting forward and shrugging into a topcoat. "No need for you to disarrange yourself; I can escort Miss Royce alone."

"Come with us, by all means," Cesare invited. "When we've left Miss Royce, I'd like to look at the path to the springs, 'Renzo—I suspect a leak in the coping."

Both men walking her home? Megan raised her eyebrows mentally, but it was certainly too soon for another "incident." Standing at the door of the guest house, she watched the brothers walking away arm in arm—'Renzo flourishing the lantern while Cesare held the umbrella—with more fraternal harmony than she'd ever seen between them. A leak in the wall coping to be inspected in the rain—*or a conference on the next plan?*

When Anna Maria had smilingly departed for the night, Megan wrapped a dressing gown about her and concentrated. What best to do? Any sensible girl would pack at once, invent an excuse, and leave tomorrow . . . and Megan had a dry hunch that there'd be at least one usable automobile to drive her to the nearest railroad station!

She even had the excuse. By now, she'd had letters from home, and she knew that Dr. Zhondek was arriving for a conference in Bologna; if Megan were still in Italy, it was imperative that she spend a few days with him and his wife. It was only a hundred miles or so, and she'd meant to persuade 'Tessa to drive down with her . . . but the events of the afternoon changed matters. It should be easy to pretend that she must meet her friends at once . . .

"I am not a sensible girl," Megan decided. "I never met this woman before in my life, but I'm damned if I'll abandon her to matricide." So—what best to do?

She would write the whole story to Uncle Joe Ames, of course. Already she'd written him something of the situation between the brothers and told him of her indignant opinion that 'Renzo was only trying to louse up things for Cesare . . . Now Megan detailed *everything*, from the trip-wire to the Cardinal's visit to today's events. It was nearly three in the morning before she finished, reread the letter carefully, signed and sealed it, and relaxed in her chair. Now what?

Once the letter was entrusted to the postal service, if anything fatal happened to her, all hell would break loose from Uncle Joe—but she must get it posted, first, *then* casually reveal that she'd written. Where to put it until she could use the runabout to mail it in Cernobbia or Como? She'd secreted the coil of wire in a pocket of a traveling bag—quietly she pulled out the bag and opened it.

The wire was gone!

Not that it would really have proved anything—but Megan sat back on her heels and for the first time felt a throb of fear. Who could have entered her bedroom without question but Anna Maria? 'Renzo or Cesare, of course. Any excuse would be acceptable to the maid, if it came from the Princes of the house . . .

Automatically, she pulled out the other bags. There was a distinct rattle in one. She snapped it open, felt the pockets with her hand and still nearly missed —because the rattle might have been the extra valise keys. It wasn't.

Cross-legged, she sat on the floor and contemplated a diamond clip. The design was ugly and old-fashioned, the stones were dirty but still faintly sparkling. "Where does this fit?" Megan scrambled to her feet, tossed another briquet onto the dwindling fire, and doused all lights but the bed lamp.

The jewel could only belong to 'Tessa, and because of the dullness of the gems, it was something she never wore. Megan went to the bathroom, ruthlessly sacrificed her toothbrush by smearing it with soap froth, gently brushed the clip under running water, and patted it dry on a towel. Little as she knew of diamonds, Megan was certain that the clip was worth a couple of thousand . . .

Why had it been planted here? Was it someone's ace in the hole, for inconvenient questions? Whom would the local police first believe: Prince 'Renzo and Cesare—or an impoverished American secretary quixotically befriended by the Contessa? Megan could imagine only too clearly the dramatic shrugs and reluctant admissions of the di Frecchias. "I hired her merely to accompany Mama to Paris; imagine my amazement to find she'd cleverly persuaded Mama to invite her to Vellanti!"

"There's no knowing when she stole the clip; she was permitted to roam at will about the castle—and to a girl of this sort, the diamonds would have seemed a fortune . . . You will notice they are of a size easily to be recut? Yes, it is surprising she had not pried them from the setting and discarded it in the lake—but what can one expect from an amateur thief, after all?"

Megan could imagine their insinuations that Mama was always easily imposed upon . . . They could easily prove that Megan was in such dire financial straits as to be tempted—perhaps there would even be a breast-beating regret that Mama should innocently have provided the temptation; but the end product would be the same: Megan Royce would be accused of murdering the Contessa in order to conceal grand larceny.

Analytically, she wondered about the legal procedure. As an American citizen accused of a capital crime, the local authorities would be forced to notify the American Ambassador . . . who would do as little as he had to, depending upon international relations between the U.S. and Italy at this moment. For Murder, though, there was a chance one of the newshounds would pick it up.

It was never going to reach that point, of course. Inadvertently, Megan had withdrawn their ace in the hole. There was still the question of where to play it: Should she tell Elise the whole story and get her to slip the thing back among 'Tessa's jewelry? The maid might suspect Megan *had* stolen it and was turning chicken because of the boathouse incident . . . Should she tell the Contessa? She'd *believe* the truth—but it might only add to her private alarms.

Take counsel in the morning, she decided, and she sleepily set the travel alarm for nine and pulled the screen across the gate. Turning, she caught a flicker between the window blinds, and automatically went to reconnoiter.

Half hidden behind the yews and shrubs of the side path was a lantern, set steady on the ground but flaring in the gusts of misty rain that still sprinkled her windows and balcony.

Megan's lips firmed. "So I'm vital enough to require surveillance?" If the watcher only knew that the latest trap had been sprung—hah! Megan quietly replaced the lifted corner of the blind and went to bed—setting both the diamond clip and her letter to Uncle Joe beneath her pillow.

CHAPTER SEVEN

As a weather forecaster, Prince Cesare was no Frank Field, Megan decided next morning. A strong breeze had blown away rain, leaving floods of sunshine and air as exhilarating as wine. It was a beautiful day, one in which to go on the water or drive somewhere with a picnic lunch—and they were immobilized at Vellanti. Megan ground her teeth at the result of her needling yesterday. She knew quite well Cesare'd only commanded the total overhaul to teach Megan a lesson. How delighted he must be that it had succeeded so well!

No thought for his mother, equally condemned to a dull day indoors or fiddling about the patio while her beloved Italy beckoned seductively. While she dressed, Megan applied herself to countering defeat. What could be devised for 'Tessa's amusement? There was the sailboat, but Megan doubted her ability to handle it alone. Ask Cesare to come with them? No, it'd be exactly what he wanted: a chance to talk to Mama alone . . . and ten to one 'Renzo would somehow include himself IN, which was exactly what Megan was trying to prevent: an opportunity to bully 'Tessa.

The village? 'Tessa would enjoy that thoroughly, from the youngest babies to the oldest grandparents, and the village would be *en fête* at sight of her!

There'd be wine and anise bread, fruit bowls and little nosegays for her to sniff. A dozen little boys would race to the fields and vineyards to say "La Contessa visits us!" and everyone would abandon his job at once. Cesare would lose a day's work while Giorgio brought out the accordion and Pietro produced his violin. "And serve Cesare right," Megan chuckled naughtily—but . . .

Could 'Tessa walk so far? The direct paths were reasonably smooth from constant use, but definitely hilly in spots. Megan thought it might be possible, with Anna Maria to take 'Tessa's other arm and plenty of rest before returning. It was that return of more than a mile downhill that bothered Megan. The Contessa was perfectly brisk, steady on her pins for all normal walking, but a rough country path was different.

Might there be a horse and cart in the village? *Of course, why didn't I think of that before!* Anna Maria would know, and Megan had a hunch that if the village knew their Contessa would visit if she were fetched and carried, they'd turn out *en masse.* Yes, it would be the perfect riposte for Cesare.

There were still the letter for Uncle Joe and the diamond clip. What best to do? Obviously she must keep the letter on her person until she could mail it. It wouldn't be safe to post this one with the Vellanti postbag; she must take NO chances now. The clip? Don't tell Elise; she's loyal to the Contessa, but no giant intellect. She might be confused and ask advice from the wrong person. Don't tell 'Tessa; she'd only be unduly distressed. "Get rid of the clip somewhere in Casa Grande, perhaps—if I can do it unobserved—in a corner of her suite."

She pinned the letter to the inside of her panty hose to lie flat across her tummy, dropped the clip into the depths of her tote bag, and went down to breakfast. "*Buon giorno*, Anna Maria. What a lovely day."

"*Sì, sì*, so good the rain stops. Where do you go today? It would be pleasant on the lake, or for a drive."

"Yes, but unfortunately there are no cars. Prince Cesare has ordered Ugo to dismantle all the motors and make certain they are safe for use," Megan said limpidly. "It is a pity the Contessa must stay at home. I thought perhaps Prince Cesare might be free to take her sailing—I cannot handle the boat alone—or perhaps she could walk as far as the village. Would there be any sort of farm cart that could bring her home?"

"*Sì, sì*," Anna Maria agreed eagerly. "There is better: my grandfather has a car, not grand but it runs well . . . and Prince Cesare is not here. He and Prince Lorenzo have gone to Milano, for business in the day and a party tonight, not to return until very, very late."

Hmmm, Megan thought grimly, *with the cats immobilized, the rats have gone out to play!* Aloud she asked, "Would your grandfather be able to spare time to drive la Contessa?"

"*Il nonno* will be honored! I call at once to arrange." She whisked away, leaving Megan pensively savoring tree-ripe oranges that needed no sugar, and contemplating the dancing blue lake. In a few minutes the maid was back with a fluffy little omelet and buttery toast. "At ten o'clock, *il nonno* arrives," she announced proudly. "He drives la Contessa to the village and wherever she wishes to go. No need to worry, he is careful driver and he can be free all day. He no longer works in the vineyards, it is very dull for the poor old man. He is *very* pleased to have something to do, Mees."

Chuckling to herself, Megan rang through to Casa Grande. "*Good* morning, 'Tessa. Isn't it a perfect day for a drive?"

"Yes, if only it were possible," the Contessa sighed faintly.

"Ah, but it is! Anna Maria has arranged everything. *Il nonno* has a car," Megan crowed. "He will come at ten, prepared to drive us anywhere and everywhere for the whole day. What d'you think of *that?*"

A moment of silence, then a tiny chuckle growing into full-throated laughter. "I think you are a witch! I was resigned to wasting this beautiful day at home, counting linens and approving the preserves in the storeroom, when one longs to be exploring old familiar sights. Where shall we go, Megan, or will you leave it to me?"

"To you, by all means, but first you will have to go to the village," Megan warned. "That will be expected, if *il nonno* is the chauffeur—and be prepared: the car is not grand but it *runs,* and *il nonno* is a careful driver."

The Contessa bubbled over again. "He is Enrico, the car will be a Fiat, and he is a careful driver—by Italian standards, Megan, which means he will frighten *you* to death, but since I am Italian, I am accustomed. Well, we will go first to the village, and then perhaps lunch at d'Este. Afterward, we will ramble along the coast to show you the views and the villas, hmmm? There will be ample time before we need be home for dinner."

"Since your sons will not be here, could it not be ordered for whenever we return?"

"*Not*—be here?" 'Tessa repeated, bewildered. "I do not understand, Megan. Where are Cesare and 'Renzo?"

"Anna Maria says they went to Milano for business, but there is a party this evening and they will not return until very late," Megan said evenly, controlling herself. When, she wondered, had 'Tessa's little darlings meant her to learn she was not merely incarcerated at Vellanti for the day but would also be alone for the night?

"Yes—yes, that is true," the Contessa murmured. "The Marinis give a gala in honor of the daughter's wedding. I, too, was invited. I declined because it is a hundred miles to go and return, too much for late at night. I thought the boys also . . . but you say they have already gone?"

"Anna Maria says so, but perhaps she was mistaken."

"No—no, I do not think she was. Well! Then we shall amuse ourselves," brightly, "and we will not miss them at all. I'll be ready at ten."

Raging inwardly, Megan rang off and pondered what more she could do to spike the princely plans. In a way, she'd already done enough. Mama would not be twiddling her fingers at Casa Grande but up-up-and-away, and when the laddies found *that* out, there'd be major perturbation! Lunch at Villa d'Este? Megan went upstairs and exchanged slacks for half-slip and skirt, tucked a pair of feminine shoes into the tote bag, and found a suitable scarf for the head.

"La Contessa is delighted," she told Anna Maria, "but after the village, she wishes to lunch at Villa d'Este and take a drive, so it may be some while before we return."

"*N'importa*," the maid shrugged. "There is no one

here waiting for you, dinner is when you arrive, *sì*? Enjoy yourselves!"

Enrico-*nonno* was drawn up before the steps of Casa Grande when Megan reached them. The Contessa with Elise behind her was just emerging. "Ah, Enrico, *buon giorno, buon giorno,*" she said with a broad smile. "It is so good of you to give me your time. I thought: the village first—and then . . ." Megan lost the rest; it was Italian too swift for her to follow, but there was no doubt of Enrico's delight in serving his Contessa.

He sprang from the Fiat (What else?) and grandly assisted 'Tessa into the rear seat with a spate of Italian that caused laughter between them. Elise hastened down to thrust a pair of white gloves (What else?) at Megan, "please to give her after luncheon."

"Yes, and please to tell no one—no one at all!—that la Contessa is not here, Elise." Megan added the gloves to her tote bag. "Remember: no matter who calls—even if it is Prince Cesare or Prince Lorenzo! La Contessa is walking in the grounds, you do not know where, please to leave a message to be given as soon as she returns. You understand?" Megan looked impersonally at the maid, whose eyes sharpened at the authoritative tone.

"*Bien sûr*, Ma'mselle." Elise nodded vigorously. She'd puzzle over such secrecy for a mere lunch and drive, but Megan did not allow for any interference. If either Cesare or 'Renzo learned Mama had flown the coop, ten to one they'd come piling back to spoil things.

"No way!" Megan said to herself firmly, hurrying into the car. Inside of two minutes she understood the Contessa's description of a "safe driver Italian style"! Enrico drove as though for the Grand Prix, with a fine flourish of horn and fancy skids at the corners, but by dint of clutching the hand strap and closing her eyes strategically, Megan shortly found herself bucketing into the main street of the village.

The Contessa smiled at her mischievously. "You see we are safe and sound. You will become accustomed." Regally assisted from the car by Enrico, she was immediately surrounded by curtseying villagers. It was *Blossomtime* and *Student Prince* all over again. An immense carved wooden chair was pantingly tugged from a nearby house by six little boys and placed in the shade of the largest tree. Other, more humble chairs were placed diffidently nearby, to which *le nonne* were graciously waved by the Contessa.

Loitering in the background, Megan was once more impressed by the simplicity, the sincerity, of these people. Cesare had said they were still feudal, and he was right. To Megan, born and bred American, it was a sort of revelation about people: no one here was a serf bound to the land; there was no one in Vellanti who could not pull up stakes and move if he thought it to his advantage—and yet they stayed happily, contentedly, respectful to a woman whose family hadn't owned them in several hundred years.

No question that it stemmed from the Contessa and her son. With no responsibility for the villagers, they were still interested in more than a day's work. Megan *noticed:* 'Tessa knew everyone by name, cooed over the babies, inquired for the health of relatives, and was deeply absorbed by local gossip. It was all Italian, of course, and too swift for Megan to catch more than a bit here or there, but 'Tessa remembered past jokes that drew delighted laughter from the crowd. There was cool fruit juice, and little cakes rushed fresh from the oven by one woman, who

106

was evidently noted for them . . . and it was all the best thing in the world for 'Tessa, Megan thought triumphantly.

It was entirely different when at length they reached the Villa d'Este. 'Tessa was suddenly Contessa di Vellanti again, nodding graciously to the maître d' ushering them to a table with a view and hovering obsequiously for the order.

"What will you like to eat, Megan?"

"Whatever you are going to have, please."

"Ah? Then," to the maître d', "we will have two Lario cocktails, the fish pâté and veal scallops in whiskey, with a green salad," she said without glancing at the menu. "Fruit and coffee later, please."

Looking out across the shimmering lake while the Contessa related all the gossip she'd gleaned, Megan was once more inwardly incredulous. "It is really I, lunching at the Villa D'Este with a contessa!" Vaguely she wondered what had happened to Bob. Los Angeles would never be anything like *this*.

"What amuses you, my dear?"

"I was apologizing to Pangloss," Megan chuckled. "Four months ago everything was the worst that could ever happen, or I thought so—and now it is completely reversed."

"The operation." 'Tessa nodded sympathetically. "Very frightening to be alone at such a time."

"Actually, it was only the black cap to climax the existing clouds," Megan said. "I'd been jilted, or thought I was, by a young opportunist who'd been using me for background until he got a good transfer to California."

"Leaving your heart broken?"

"Not really. It was mostly my pride," Megan admitted. "He didn't take my money or anything like

107

that, he had a very good salary and paid his own way, but—but he encouraged me to spend all I had for an apartment I couldn't afford." Encouraged by the Contessa's gentle interest, she put it all into words, and—amazingly—it began to fall into place.

"I shouldn't really blame Bob," she reflected. "He simply took advantage of my naïveté. I *assumed* we were to marry, and he didn't correct me. Besides, I enjoyed every minute of premières and first nights and press parties—planning dinners and meeting the sort of people I'd never known. It was exciting and glamorous, I learned a great deal about—oh, money and how to behave among strangers or at top restaurants.

"It's not a life I'd like, I'm not very competitive," she murmured, looking vaguely across the lake. "My father was an accountant with a famous firm, and you know what that means: they work every day of the year. Mother had a rheumatic heart; we lived a very quiet life. There was always enough money, I went to Smith with no financial strain, and of course I met girls who traveled, whose families had opera subscriptions and so on—but between Daddy's job and Mother's heart, we didn't.

"When Father died, there was still enough money. We thought of selling the house and moving to an apartment in Manhattan that would be easier for me with my job, but I knew Mother'd miss her garden and the neighbors. Then," Megan's voice trembled, "she died, too, and I made a fool of myself."

"Women always do at one time or another, my dear." Tessa smiled wryly. "It is part of life. You are fortunate to have got it out of the way when you are so young. As you say, you have learned a bit of the superficial world. It will be useful when you marry.

You will have the famed American 'Know-how,' if he becomes the president of IBM."

"Heaven forbid," Megan protested, laughing. "Can you imagine *me* having to buy gowns in Paris?"

"No, you would not like it at all," 'Tessa agreed, straight-faced. "We must hope it does not occur, but if it does, I will teach you. It would be worth—what is the expression—'the price of admission' to see you coping with the arrogance of Givenchy or St Laurent!" She laughed helplessly. "You would win, but the fray would leave everyone but the spectators exhausted."

"Oh, dear, I'm not a fighter," Megan sighed. "Let's hope all the corporation presidents are already married."

"I feel sure they are." 'Tessa raised an eyebrow to a nearby waiter and the maître d' slithered forward with the bill discreetly face down on a silver plate. "However, they are today's presidents, and who knows what young men may succeed them, Megan."

"You mean it'd be my luck to marry someone who was going right to the White House?"

"Perhaps," the Contessa nodded, dropping notes on the salver. "I think it unlikely, you are not aggressive enough, my dear, but if it turned out that way—do not doubt yourself. You would do it very well. What I wonder," she added pensively, pushing away from the table and rising with gracious smiles for waiter and sommelier, "what I wonder is how this Bob has explained your absence beside him in his new position."

"Why should he have to?" Megan asked, astonished, following her hostess to the exit. "He's in California. Nobody there would know my name."

"Oh, they do, my dear—they do." The Contessa smiled at her wickedly. "You and your dinner parties

109

are one reason the young man got his transfer. I may be Italian, my dear Megan, but I know very well the ways of American business. There will be people from New York coming out for conferences who will say, 'Where is Miss Royce? When do you marry?' It would be amusing to hear his replies. Has he pretended you are a career woman who never wished to leave her job, that this was always understood between you? I must tell you that I do not think it would answer. There will be far too many who recall your attitude as hostess, deferring to the man soon to be head of the house.

"They will not for a minute believe you the career woman! Bob will have to think of another excuse," 'Tessa chuckled, sauntering forward to the Fiat that Enrico was arrogantly whizzing to the entrance in front of a Rolls Royce and a Mercedes Benz. "I am surprised you have not heard from him—but you will, *cara* Megan. You will!"

"He doesn't know where I am."

"Surely you left a forwarding address?" 'Tessa shrugged, as Enrico grandly opened the car door. "'Rico, you have had a good lunch? *Buono!* Now I come in front beside you—you do not mind? But please not to drive too quickly. I wish to *see* everything, *comprendi?*"

"*Sì, sì,* Contessa. Szirbino, *forse?*" The old man bustled forward to open the front seat, beaming with pleasure that la Contessa should sit beside him, and leaving Megan to insert herself in the rear unassisted.

She did not mind, she had plenty to think about while 'Tessa and Enrico gossiped in swift Italian. She had *not* left any forwarding address at the post office; the apartment superintendent and his wife were unusually responsible. "I do not know where I shall be. If there is any emergency you can call Dr. Innisperg or Dr. Ames, but otherwise would you simply clear the box? Read the magazines and discard when you've finished. Throw out the junk mail, and send any personal letters to Dr. Innisperg. He'll always know where I am."

And so he did, via weekly postcards from Megan; she'd already had a slim envelope containing a few letters from college friends and a chatty note from the other secretaries. Nothing from Bob; there never had been anything from Bob since he'd left the keys and huffed out of the apartment. As of now, he not only didn't know she was in Europe, but was unaware of the appendectomy. Megan pondered the Contessa's prediction: Could it be true, was Bob finding surprise at the lack of Megan?

More probably he'd found another little goose to hostess for him, she thought cynically. All the same, she felt troubled if it might somehow affect his job. He didn't, she decided, deserve that. Now that she'd examined it in telling 'Tessa, Bob had been a bit of a cad, but also he had given her some social polish that made her acceptable to a rich aristocratic family. Should Megan write to him? After four months of silence, what to say? Might he not think she was trying to "get him back"?

"No way!" Megan's mind said instantly. "Can't think what I ever saw in him—but I'd like him to know it, to know I wasn't crushed." As Enrico whirled grandly in Szirbino, it was decided: she would write. Let Bob have a story for any questioners—*and let me have a little bitchery, I deserve that much.*

Cesare's model community was entirely different from Vellanti. The cottages were simple but well constructed of uniform design. To Megan, it was an Italian version of Levittown, and as they drove slowly along the central road, she found it depressing. She reminded herself it was a new colony—unfair to compare with a home village where trees and shrubs had flourished for a century. A central communal square was well sodded for *boccie*, and floodlit for evening games, although it was in active use by a number of young men.

Unemployment? It was known to be high in Italy, but surely there was enough land to the rear of the cottages for these men to be working a vineyard or growing some sort of crops.

Beside the *boccie* lawn was a small general store to the left, a modest *taverna* to the right, with some tables for onlookers and the ubiquitous Coca-Cola machine. It seemed a sort of local club. Mothers gossiped over bottles of Coke, babies napped in carrycots or crawled about in a fenced play area to the rear. Enrico idled the car along and loudly hailed one of the *boccie* players with a vigorous wave of his hand. "Arturo, *come sta?* It is my nephew," he explained to 'Tessa.

"Ah? Let us stop, then."

For perhaps twenty minutes, the Contessa sauntered about, but it was not Vellanti. There was no discourtesy, but these were not freehold cottagers with a lineage of respect for the Family. Here there were tenants, and as always, with complaints for dilatory repairs and clogged pipes.

"Drano," said Megan oracularly to the Contessa, who looked startled. "It's a liquid that opens drainpipes. Don't you know these women shampoo in the kitchen sink, and if you look at their mops! The amount of hair must be horrendous."

112

"I never heard of it," 'Tessa murmured blankly.

"You wouldn't have," Megan said kindly, "but it works, or you can get a sort of suction thing—a plunger, I think. Any supermarket has them."

"In Italy?"

"Perhaps not," Megan conceded. "I remember the only thing Mme. Bérard took home from New York was a dozen large boxes of Brillo; she insisted it was not available in Paris. Anyway, I'll write Mrs. Innisperg to send some Drano, and when the signoras see how well it works, they'll get it imported, you'll see."

"Is your Italian good enough to give a small lecture?" 'Tessa inquired, seriously. "House management, cleaning aids, and so on? I'll try to interpret."

Megan gulped, "Well, I'll do my best, but if you never heard of Drano, I don't know how far we'll get."

They got quite a long way. The men returned to *boccie*, but a number of the women tagged behind Megan and the Contessa, who explored a few cottages. It was totally unfamiliar for Megan, but she threw up her chin and outlined American housekeeping methods to an increasingly eager questioning period. She grew reckless as time passed, because she had been partly right in her early naughty assessment of a Development for poor people—but also Prince Cesare had done an excellent job of planning.

"I wonder what he means to do next," she said impulsively as they climbed back into the car.

"You think it worth continuing?"

Megan nodded. "Most of the tenants are trying, 'Tessa. They want to be clean and tidy, but they either don't know how or haven't money for soap or wax. The others are either natural slatterns who wouldn't really be comfortable without squalor, or they're defeated by too many children and not enough anything else. I suppose if you have a husband out of work, and six babies, you'd easily go under."

"Yes," 'Tessa murmured cryptically, "but what to do?"

"In Italy, I wouldn't know," Megan said after a moment. "Maybe some sort of cottage industry? Or a day-care center so the women could go to work— if there is any. Doesn't your son have any ideas?"

"I believe he does." 'Tessa nodded, and deliberately changed the subject. "How pleasant to see so many boats on the lake . . . and there is Isola Comacina. Another day we will lunch there, when someone can take us in the launch . . . and here is Villa Arconati. I must telephone to see if any of the family is there. They are Americans. You would like them, Megan, and the villa is supremely beautiful. Now we come to Tremezzo—not so *fast*, 'Rico! We wish to *see*!"

"*Perdono*, Contessa . . ."

"Beyond is the Villa Carlotta—the gardens are incomparable, it is acknowledged throughout the world," 'Tessa said proudly. "A hundred years ago Stendhal wrote of those gardens, but they are even more beautiful today.

"Another day we will drive through Como and up to Bellagio. There is the Villa Melzi; its grounds are very formal and English. That is where Liszt stayed with his mistress until their daughter Cosima was born."

"Goodness, how romantic! With that background, no wonder she ran off with Wagner," Megan exclaimed, peering about at the villas lining the road beside them. "So tantalizing to see only tilted roofs and glimpses of the lakeside. Didn't anyone build on the hills, like Vellanti?"

"A great many families," 'Tessa nodded. "I will show you one. 'Rico, *prego,* take us to the palazzo."

"*Sì,* Contessa."

Lost in the views of lake and villas, Megan had no idea of time, but suddenly they were drawn up before imposing scrolled iron gates with a small gatehouse. At 'Rico's imperious horn, a man emerged, but he merely shook his head when requested to open. "*Il Principe* says no one, but *no one,* is to enter! No tourists, no one to view," he insisted stubbornly.

Enrico descended from the car and went forward. "WHAT is this?" he demanded. "Here is la Contessa, Principessa di Frecchia, la mama of Prince Lorenzo— and *she* is not to be admitted? *Stupido!* It is only tourists he wishes to keep away."

"I do not know, only that no one is to enter." The man became uncertain. "I have not had word that *la Principessa* visits, I have only my orders, and how do I know you tell the truth?"

"And how do we know *you* tell the truth?" 'Rico's lip curled. "The prince goes to Milano for a day, you close the gates with this tale of orders, but for *una mancia,* you consent to open, eh?"

"No, no, it is not so! I do not want the bribe!"

"Be quiet, Enrico." The Contessa leaned forward. "Where is Ruggiero? Who are you?"

"I am Aldo; Ruggiero grows old, he is retired." The gatekeeper hesitated. "*Perdono,* Principessa—if that is who you are—but one has one's orders. I was not told . . . and I have never seen you before."

"No, it is some years since I was last here," she said with an effort. "I live much in America these days. I had not heard that Ruggiero was retired, but I should have realized. He must be nearly eighty."

"Eighty-one next year," Aldo returned automatically,

"but very well for his age. Eh, if I knew what best to do . . ."

"What is best is to open the gates for la Principessa," 'Rico stated.

"Wait! Are there tenants?" the Contessa asked.

"No, no, they do not arrive yet. There is no one but two maids and a gardener."

"Flora and Pauline?" At his nod, "Then it can do no harm to admit us, Aldo. You need say nothing, I will make all straight with Prince Lorenzo tonight."

Her recognition of the maid's names decided Aldo. The gates were rolled back, the Fiat rolled forward and turned up a winding approach drive with a profusion of flowers on either side, but even to Megan's suburban eyes, the grounds were faintly unkempt. The sward badly needed mowing, the privet was untrimmed, and the shrubs wanted pruning. The Contessa sat silent, her face strained with control and all her earlier enjoyment gone.

Frecchia was a true palazzo in contrast to the villas Megan had seen along their road. It was far more grand than Vellanti, with numerous outbuildings half hidden behind trees in the rear, and great carved doors worthy of a *duomo*. These were open, with two elderly maids eagerly waiting for the Contessa with curtseys and a flood of excited Italian. "Ah, if only we had known! Aldo calls, but already you are ascending the drive."

"*N'importa*—a sudden whim—please not to disarrange yourselves," 'Tessa said mechanically. "I should like to take Miss Royce to see some of the rooms—no need for you to leave your work, we do not stay long."

"*Sì, sì*, you know your way!"

Megan followed 'Tessa in growing bewilderment. The rooms were not dirty, which was a tribute to Flora and Pauline, but two elderly women could never possibly keep all the chandeliers and bibelots sparkling. Perhaps the palazzo was only fully maintained when there were tenants?

"The grand salon . . . the state dining room . . . the library . . ." From one to another they went, and finally ascended the wide marble staircase, to walk along halls and peer briefly into bedchambers. Here and there Megan was aware of blank spaces on walls, of an oddly barren mantelshelf or a makeshift muslin coverlet upon a majestic tester bed, but only when they reached what was obviously the master's chamber did she realize.

The Contessa entered, and after a swift glance, half staggered. Megan grasped her elbow and steered her to a chair. She was alarmingly white-faced. "It is nothing, merely—memories," she murmured.

Looking about, Megan thought the reality of today compared to 'Tessa's past sight of this room might well be agitating. Like the others, it was not dirty—merely unattended. The lusters of the wall sconces were dull, so were the brass firedogs. A handsome rococo clock sat on the mantel, but there was a huge discolored patch on the wall behind it.

The Contessa glanced about once more and rose. "I should not have come, he did mean to keep me out," she murmured distractedly. "There are more rooms, but—another day, Megan. Let us go."

In the salon there was wine and little fried cakes hastily contrived by the maids to honor la Principessa —impossible to refuse, although Megan sensed it was taking all 'Tessa's fortitude to be seated, to be gracious,

to inquire for the families of the servants. As if in
sympathy with distress, the sky suddenly darkened
with a presage of rain.

"I think we should go, 'Tessa," Megan suggested.
"Perhaps we can get home before the storm."

"*Sì, sì,*" the maids agreed, rushing about to close
the long windows. "Ah, so quickly it blows up from
the lake! Best to leave at once, Principessa . . .
arrivederci, arrivederci . . . so joyful to see you!"

They returned to Vellanti at high speed and in
silence. Stealing a glance at the Contessa's somber
face, Megan's heart was wrung by its misery. Enrico
did not linger at Casa Grande. "It was my pleasure,
Contessa. Send word any time!" The heavens opened
exactly as Megan and her hostess were inside.

"We made it." Megan tried for cheerfulness. "Thanks
for a lovely day, 'Tessa."

"But it is not over yet." 'Tessa turned to stare down
at her from the stairs. "Please—let us have wine or tea
or *something* . . . or are you too tired, Megan? Forgive me, I forget you have been ill. It is only that I
am—restless. In any case, you cannot go to Casa Piccola in this rain. Come with me, Elise will find a
caftan for you . . ."

"*I'm* not at all tired," Megan disclaimed, "but I
thought perhaps you'd like to lie down or be alone
for a while. I could sit in the salon, or perhaps there's
a poncho for me to get down the hill."

"*No!*" The great dark eyes were bleak, pleading
wildly. "No, I do not want to be alone!"

"Then you needn't be." Megan swiftly went up to
put her arm about the older woman for assistance.

"It was only—so many changes I had not realized,"
'Tessa said in a low voice. "I do not want to think
just yet, it would be good to sit quietly before the

fire until dinner, and if the rain does not stop, you shall stay the night here."

"Very well, that sounds attractive." Megan strove for a gay note. "Nothing's better for a rainy evening than comfortable clothes and gossip, or a cutthroat game of gin rummy. It makes you feel *almost* superior to God: 'You meant to ruin our day, but see how ingenious Your children are! Here we sit laughing, while Your storm passes by!'"

'Tessa smiled faintly. "That is a novel way to look at it. Ah, Elise, please find some sort of robe or caftan for Miss Royce, and I will have a housecoat and slippers. Were there any events during the day?"

"A few telephone calls: Signora Duanti wishes you to lunch next Tuesday, the Duchessa degli Carnese asks you to phone when you have the time, and Prince Cesare called from Milano to ask if he could bring you anything," Elise said placidly, with a side glance at Megan. "I said you were out with Mlle. Royce, I did not know where, and reminded Prince Cesare you were particularly fond of the pistachio nougat."

Wonder what he really wanted? Megan thought, taking the green silk caftan Elise produced and rapidly stripping off blouse and skirt. *No word from 'Renzo?* If the boys were in it together, perhaps it was enough for one of them to check on Mama. Fumbling in the bottom of her tote bag, her fingers encountered the diamond clip beside her comb.

Here was the golden opportunity. In a twinkling she'd silently pushed it into a pigeonhole of the escritoire. There'd be loud amazement when it was found, but at least it was back with its owner. There remained the letter to Uncle Joe, still pinned to her panty hose. She'd had no chance to get a stamp unobserved by the Contessa, who would wonder why it had not been left for Ugo to give the postman. Equally to ask Anna Maria to bring a stamp would cause surprise. *Better not . . .* but it was a major problem: not merely necessary to get a stamp, but to find a postbox somewhere unobserved. *There has to be a way—think later.*

When 'Tessa emerged in a stunning velvet robe embellished with lace frills at neck and wrists, she looked more calm. "I have been thinking," she announced. "We meant to consult Elena for her recipes. Why not now? It will serve to occupy our minds until dinner time."

In the kitchen, the Contessa perched on a stool and interpreted whenever Megan got into difficulties. Elena was enchanted to be consulted by Mees, willingly parted with anything and everything to the accompaniment of a tisane and pound cake still warm from the oven. It was excellent therapy for the Contessa. Their struggle with cookery terms that were equally unfamiliar whether Italian or English produced gales of mirth, until she looked herself again.

In the middle of everything, Ugo threw open the rear door. He was rain-soaked, obviously tired and dour as always, and flabbergasted to see the Contessa and Megan happily bent over the kitchen table. *"Perdono!"*

He made as if to back away, but 'Tessa said quickly, "It's all right, Ugo; we're just leaving. Come in, dry yourself. Have you finished?"

"Sì, Contessa," he grunted. "The boat is ready for Mees. Tomorrow I finish the motors."

"I can use the runabout tomorrow then? Thank you, Ugo!" He ducked his head ungraciously and vanished along the servants' hall while Megan collected her papers and slid down from the stool. Following 'Tessa out to the main hall, Megan asked involuntarily, "What's with Ugo? He's the only person in all of Vellanti who seems not to like anyone."

"And you wonder why we keep him?" The Contessa smiled. "His family has been with us for hundreds of years, but even more, he was with 'Renzo in the Underground. 'Renzo saved his life, but while Ugo was away, his only daughter was raped and killed by the Germans. We never forget that, but I suppose Ugo never forgets it, either." She sighed. "It is sad, but in his own way, he is devoted to us."

CHAPTER EIGHT

There was still rain, but the wind had died. Megan and 'Tessa sat in the salon and talked of impersonal things. It was principally Megan, but her stories of the men, the girls in the office, the neighbors in her apartment house—all were lively and amusing. By now, the Contessa knew the names and asked questions, laughing but deeply interested in the answers.

"Innisperg—that is an odd name. From where does he come?"

"Nebraska, but I suppose originally it may have been Swedish," Megan considered. "He's a geologist by accident. He meant to be an English professor, but he took a makeweight college course, only to fill out his schedule—and he was so intrigued, he switched his major . . . and now he's one of the top men in the world!"

"Which only proves how wise it may be to change in midstream," 'Tessa nodded, "as with this Bob, for instance. I think you are well out of it—Los Angeles is not attractive. The smog is worse than in New York, and one grows tired of constant sunshine."

"*Perdono,* Contessa—at what hour does Mees wish to retire?"

"Oh, tonight she will sleep here, Ugo. No need for

you to wait," the Contessa said. "Go along to your bed when you choose, *buon sonno.*"

"*Grazie . . .*"

But after all, Megan did go back to Casa Piccola to sleep. The rain had dwindled to a fine mist, the Contessa opted for early bed, and looking from the guest room, Megan could see lights in Casa Piccola. Anna Maria was probably waiting for her. Impulsively, she changed back to her blouse and skirt, and let herself out of the front door to pick up one of the waiting lanterns. She got back quite safely, only slightly damp from brushing against shrubbery.

Anna Maria exclaimed in horror, "Why did you not call? I would have come with the rainclothes. I draw a bath at once to prevent any taking cold, and bring some hot coffee."

"I'm not really wet," Megan laughed, "but a bath will be nice." She rang through to Elise, "I came home —tell la Contessa tomorrow?"

"*Oui*—but I would have called Ugo. Why did you not ask?"

"Oh, it's late, and he's worked hard all day. Let him have a good night's sleep, and perhaps he'll finish the automobile motors tomorrow. *Bon soir, dormez bien.*"

Refreshed by the bath and furnished with a large cup of piping hot cappuccino laced with rum, Megan sent Anna Maria to bed. "I shall write a letter, and I'll adjust blinds and windows for myself," she smiled. "*Buon sònno.*"

Reconnoitering from the window, she saw there was no watcher tonight. Well, that figured. The princes were sashaying about a dance floor fifty miles away, and everybody else thought she was staying at Casa Grande for the night . . . yet who could have been standing guard over her, and why? One point was settled: tomorrow she'd mail the letter to Uncle Joe somewhere along the lake, since the runabout was usable.

Sipping the coffee, Megan thought back over the day. It had been delightful—until they reached Palazzo di Frecchia. 'Tessa had loved her visit to the village, had enjoyed the lunch at Villa D'Este. Had the visit to Szirbino been a mistake? Personally, Megan thought Prince Cesare was doing rather well with his development, but perhaps it had only reminded 'Tessa that he wanted *money* to continue. *Her* money . . .

"Darn it, I was supposed to be buffer state," Megan sighed. "I shouldn't have let her stop there . . ." but it was 'Rico who'd suggested it, and during the later drive 'Tessa had been quite happy. It was only the visit at Frecchia that changed everything. True that the palazzo hadn't looked spruce and magnificent, but if 'Renzo had known she'd be coming, he'd have had it in shape . . . or would he?

Why was he staying at Vellanti instead of occupying a suite in his own home? Well, Frecchia was a powerful lot of rooms to be rattling about in alone . . . but if he rented most of the year, why not a paint job inside? Was that why 'Renzo wanted money? A thousand bucks would do the main rooms in America; in Italy he could probably do the whole place—and to his Mama, that would be a pittance.

The longer she thought, the more baffling. Megan abandoned it finally. She wrote to Mrs. Innisperg, asking for Drano and some other standard American supplies, she finished the coffee, and went to bed.

The wind changed during the night, taking the rain with it, but when Megan awoke to brilliant crisp sunshine, nothing spoke to her of what the wind might have brought in replacement for the rain that day. Blithely, she waved to Anna Maria and went to the boathouse. The hole in the planking was still there, but readied for repair, the broken boards neatly removed and a criss-cross of slats nailed to prevent anyone's inadvertently walking into that corner. The runabout bobbed gently in its berth, filled with petrol as always; someone was apparently in charge of immediate refill at Vellanti, for Megan had never found the tank less than full.

Her letter to Uncle Joe was sealed securely in a waterproof bag. She'd go to Cernobbia, to Como if time permitted, but she would mail it unobserved. Once the letter was on its way, she could concentrate on protecting 'Tessa . . . although Megan admitted to herself there was no future to the situation. She couldn't stay at Vellanti forever. Even if she stayed until the Contessa departed, now that murder had once been tried, it could be tried again, any time, any place.

Time was actually no longer a factor, because whichever way the Contessa decided, her sons had each other by the short hairs; neither could back out of the conspiracy merely because he'd got his. The only solution would be to catch 'em in the act, to drag it into the open with proof. Then Mama could disinherit her cherubs of course, but if it had to be a police matter, Megan suspected Contessa Giulia Vellanti di Frecchia Waldron would almost rather let her sons kill her.

Suppose she gave them their inheritance outright? It would restrict her living standards drastically, but on the other hand, 'Tessa was not a socially active young woman. She already had the luxurious furs and jewels; she no longer spent thousands a year on Paris gowns; she was entirely content to divide her time between a wing of the Waldron ranch house and hotel suites in New York, London, or Rome. She was happy to visit with old friends, entertain informally, and enjoy opera and symphony subscriptions. In fact, she never spent all her income on herself; most of it went to charity—suppose she decided that charity begins at home?

Megan had no idea of 'Tessa's finances, but surely it should be possible for her to live comfortably on a third of her current income, if she stopped charitable contributions. Would the Contessa wish to purchase her life in this way? "That's her problem, not yours," Megan told herself, tying up to the end of the Cernobbia landing and hopping out to face a majestic harbor assistant. "Is it all right for me to occupy this space while I post a letter?" she asked in careful Italian—and added a naïve dimple for good measure.

It was more than all right; it was an honor, and 'Vanni Montoro ("at your service, signorina") would be enchanted to check the gas supply.

Swinging along the harbor street to the post office, Megan thought that there definitely was *something* about the Italian male reaction to females! Coming out of the building, she met the delivery man for Vellanti, who was delighted to chat for a minute. "You would like to take the mail, perhaps?"

"I meant to go on to Como," she said dubiously.

The man shrugged casually. "You will still reach Vellanti before me," he said. He sorted through the mail bags and extended a double handful of letters. "So many papers, circulars, magazines—so many villas, and all the cottages; *Dio mio!* You could go to the moon and still be at Vellanti before me!"

"All right; *grazie!*" Megan stuffed everything into her tote bag and with a wave of the hand trotted back to the boat, where "At Your Service" Montoro strode forward reproachfully. "I'm sorry, but I met the Vellanti postman; how could I ignore him, after all?"

"You are from Vellanti? This you did not say, signorina! Ah, that is altogether a different matter . . ."

"I only meant to stay fifteen minutes," she explained. But "Vellanti" was a magic word, and even in Cernobbia it was known that an American "Mees" was visiting la Contessa. 'Vanni Montoro was not minded to miss his opportunity of firsthand acquaintance! The entire boat was checked and rechecked instantly, while Megan received masses of useless information concerning various places she had no intention of visiting. Eventually, he stepped back to the dock, assuring her that all was in order, but should difficulties arise, Mees had only to pull in at Cernobbia, where 'Vanni Montoro would be ever at her service.

"Oh, thank you so much!" Megan left him standing magnificently erect, a hand raised in farewell.

She managed to round the point before she giggled . . .

In Como, she was efficiently directed to a side landing; the harbor master was polite but brisk. He collected her lire impersonally, but he unbent slightly when the captain of the boat for Lecco tooted and waved as Megan turned up to the town. For a full hour she rambled about, seeing what was to be seen and window shopping. Eventually she went back to the boat, buying a basket of fresh purple figs for 'Tessa, who confessed a passion for them. It was too early for Vellanti figs; these were Calabrian, but they

127

seemed exactly ripe and just the sort of tiny present to please her hostess.

She was back in the boathouse by one, phoning Elise to apologize for lateness. "*Ce n'est rien; M'dame est en retard aussi . . . on a commandé déjeuner à deux heures . . .*"

"Oh, good, I'll be there by two!" Holding the basket of figs carefully, Megan circled around the servant's entrance and dramatically set them before Elena. "*Por la Contessa!*"

Italians never do anything the easy way; there was instant jubilation, congratulations. "Where did you find them?" Elena cried. "Ah, how pleased la Contessa will be! Today everyone thinks of her, Mees; see— there are fresh wood mushrooms, too!"

Elena tilted the small plaited rush basket and spilled them magnificently across the kitchen table— and Megan caught her breath, staring wide-eyed, while the cook proudly described how they would be cooked, "to a tenderness, *signorina,* to a tenderness! A hint of garlic, a whisper of paprika, plenty of fresh parsley, and a suggestion of nutmeg. Ah, it is too bad Adri does not find more than enough for la Contessa, but," she ran on anxiously, "you will understand, Mees? It is a favorite dish, a specialty she particularly enjoys, and there is not enough if one tries to share."

"Of course I understand," Megan said mechanically, still conscious of shock—for at the bottom of the basket were three superb specimens, each with a delicate, enticing orange gill. They were *amanitas, deadly poisonous toadstools* . . . Surely Megan couldn't be wrong, couldn't have forgotten her father's teaching in those long-ago days when they'd ranged the Vermont woods during vacations?

As Elena's hand moved to collect the fungi into a pan, Megan came out of her trance and swiftly extracted the amanitas—but were the others edible? "Who is Adri?" Megan asked.

"The son of 'Nesto, who cares for the greenhouses." Elena's hand hesitated, her dark eyes questioning. "He is only seven years old, but already he knows much of growing things," she muttered, eyeing the toadstools Megan had set aside.

"Yes, those are poisonous," Megan told her quietly, "and I'm sorry, Elena, but I don't know enough to be sure about the others, either."

In one fell swoop, the mushrooms and toadstools were in the garbage pail. "We take no chances! I confess, I am city-bred, I would not know. Thank the good God you were here, Mees! So often and often they bring me fungi," Elena said distractedly, "and always it is all right, always la Contessa eats and enjoys. Prince Cesare himself brings me a handful and says, 'Elena, *por desinare* . . .'" She was half crying, and Megan pulled herself together.

"Elena, *parl-'nièntel*" she said authoritatively. "It was an accident, a little boy wanting only to give pleasure."

"True—but what to say?"

"Tell him la Contessa ate every one, enjoyed them thoroughly, asked you to thank him from the bottom of her heart! Why make a little boy unhappy?"

"*Sì, una gentilezza . . .*"

"More than that," Megan said urgently, "tell *no one*—no one at all, Elena. Not Ugo, nor Prince Cesare, nor Ma'mselle Elise, *not anyone at all*, you understand?" The cook stared at her blankly and shook her head. "Don't you see," Megan went on softly, "if you tell *anyone* . . . they won't be able to resist whispering to someone else! Before long, it gets back to Adri's family—and perhaps they would even *beat* him!"

"Oh, assuredly . . ."

"But la Contessa would not like him whipped for a mistake like that. After all, it harmed no one," Megan wheedled. "So if anyone should ask, no matter *who*, you will say you cooked Adri's basket of mushrooms and the Contessa enjoyed them! *Convenuto?*"

"*Sì, sì,*" Elena agreed heartily. "You are absolutely right, Mees—ah, you have the good heart for a child, because me—I tell you, that 'Nesto has a quick tongue, a harsh hand, and the boy is not robust. I say nothing!"

"In America, we shake hands for an agreement, so we will not forget what we have promised." Megan held out her hand, drawing herself erect and looking very serious. Elena wiped her hand on her apron and slapped it dramatically into Megan's—and for good measure, she crossed herself simultaneously, after which she frowned slightly and said, "But if there are no fungi, there must be something else . . ."

"An omelet, a plain salad, the figs? There's plenty of time," Megan smiled. "I shall talk to la Contessa for a while . . ."

"Second try," Megan told herself coldly, as she came into the main hall. Involuntarily, she leaned against the great marble newel post, swept by a wave of sheer terror. What had she undertaken to do? How could she hope to do it, if the di Frecchias were this clever? It was pure chance she'd been in the kitchen at a crucial moment.

Otherwise, the Contessa would have been served a delicate dish of fresh sautéed mushrooms, lovingly prepared by Elena . . . Unquestionably, she'd have insisted that Megan taste at least one or two—and by this evening, 'Tessa would be *in extremis,* while Megan might (or might not) have vomited sufficiently to be limp but alive. And a seven-year-old child would have been tagged with murdering, through childish ignorance, the woman he'd wanted only to please.

The cool marble against her forehead collected her thoughts. Never mind the callous disregard that could ruin a child's life—could Megan turn it to good account? If Elena kept her mouth shut . . . Well, she wouldn't, of course, but perhaps she'd keep the secret for a few days. If Megan could make friends with Adri, persuade him to show her where he'd found the mushrooms . . . *and learn whom he had met on his way to the castle with his gift for la Contessa . . .*

It had been Cesare, of course, Megan thought sick- ly, dragging herself slowly up the steps—Cesare, who knew enough about fungi to be able to bring a hand- ful to Elena for his own dinner now and then . . . and who'd have no trouble inserting the poisonous amanitas beneath the boy's mushrooms while the child quested for more.

Now what? Megan tightened her lips grimly. She would go down to Cernobbia tomorrow morning, buy a basket of local mushrooms, and get Elena to present them for la Contessa's luncheon, saying these were from Adri! That would be one in the eye all round, because 'Tessa was sure to make a point of thanking Adri in person—and as long as Elena could be kept quiet, the murderers would be totally in the dark!

And bully for our side! *"Bonjour, Elise, c'est moi . . . ça va?"* Good morning, 'Tessa, did you sleep well?" Megan had the answer before she bent to hug the

131

older woman—in the Contessa's strained dark eyes, white face, the shadowed cheekbones. What could have happened unknown to Megan? "I went all the way to Como this morning and collected the mail at Cernobbia," she announced gaily, hauling the wad of papers and letters from her tote bag and dropping them on the side table. "Oh, a letter from Uncle Joe! Elise, *je vous prie, mon ange,* sort the rest?"

The sprawling medical-prescription fly tracks of Dr. Ames's handwriting took concentration, and the subject matter took even more . . . because in the course of his Park Avenue practice Uncle Joe had stumbled on something: Prince Lorenzo di Frecchia was a hairbreadth from total bankruptcy, including loss of the Frecchia estates!

"I got this direct from the pig's mouth," wrote Uncle Joe, "said pig being an oily bit of Arkansas who's proud to trace his ancestry to a carpetbagger and even prouder to have an Italian prince by the short hairs. On appearance, Mrs. Pig's ancestry stems from Polly Adler. I suspect a nasty mess brewing. Enclosed, a check for $500. Please leave at once, Megan. I don't want you involved in an international scandal; your reputation would survive, but your physical health will not."

Very quietly, Megan folded letter and check into the envelope. This was the most alarming development so far. All along, Megan had supposed 'Renzo had merely been throwing his weight around out of sibling rivalry and a desire to annoy his brother—but his need was actually more desperate than Cesare's. Did his mother know it? Obviously not—or she'd have paid up at once to save the family estates . . . But why hadn't 'Renzo told the truth when his first gambit of "expanding the business" failed? That would have meant too much loss of face, of course; 'Renzo was a small man . . .

Slitting open the other letter Elise had dropped in her lap, Megan suddenly realized that Uncle Joe's news had a good side: it settled the time limit. If foreclosure were imminent, 'Renzo probably had no more than a couple of weeks in which to murder his mother and prevent disclosure. If 'Tessa could be protected only for that length of time, the jig would be up for 'Renzo, and there'd be no point in murder. Could Megan manage that?

Apparently she could! Dr. Innisperg wrote that the Zhondeks would arrive in Milan Friday next, and he insisted Megan join them as their guest, to be company for Mme. Zhondek while Serge attended the Bologna conference. Furthermore, he'd just learned that an old college friend of Mrs. Innisperg's was married to the doctor attached to the U.S. embassy in Rome.

Perfect! Megan must somehow persuade the Contessa to join the safari to Bologna, then get her to Rome and the Embassy doctor . . . That would keep her out of 'Renzo's reach until the fat caught fire.

"How much does it cost to telephone Rome?" Megan asked. "My boss has given me the name of a friend to get in touch with . . ."

"It isn't expensive, but you can't call today, I'm afraid," the Contessa answered. "It seems our phones are not working for outside calls."

"What a shame I didn't know; I could have reported it in Cernobbia!"

"That would have been useless, I fear," the Contessa smiled dryly. "Italian repairmen are—leisurely. No doubt the phones will be operating in a day or so, but meanwhile we seem to be rather isolated. I'm sorry, my dear, but at least you have the boat to amuse you until Ugo reassembles the motors."

"I'm surprised they let him finish that," Megan muttered without thinking—but the Contessa did not pretend to misunderstand.

"If they'd known you would collect the mail, I expect the boat would have needed a replacement part."

Megan drew a long breath. "So you *do* know. Well, it isn't going to happen, but you have to get away from here; you know that?"

"That would not be permitted; *you* know that. I'm not even certain you'll be allowed to leave—now."

"Why not? They can't risk anything odd—and after Ugo said in front of Elena yesterday that the boat was ready, and Mees has been seen the length of Lake Como all morning . . . it would be extremely odd for the boat to be decommissioned a few hours later." Megan chuckled. "You'd never muffle Elena —she'd tell the entire village that Ugo is slipping and can't even mend an engine!"

"Yes," 'Tessa said, suddenly thoughtful, "it's worth a try. After lunch I will write letters; if all goes well, you will post them in Cernobbia for me . . . and now we must contrive to place the rest of the mail in its usual place." She looked directly at Megan. "*That* is the danger spot—if anyone should know the mail reached me before it was—inspected . . ."

"I never realized—I've received *my* letters . . ."

"But I have not, and by today's post, it's obvious some of my outgoing letters have been—lost."

There was a knock at the door of the sitting room. "Luncheon for la Contessa," Ugo announced from the hall.

"Delay him a minute!" Megan hissed to Elise, as

she sprang to shuffle all the mail into her tote bag. Rapidly, she seized the Contessa's opened letters and thrust them into a drawer, adding the unopened ordinary mail to her bag. "Now—*you* delay Ugo until I get rid of this. Pretend I haven't arrived yet . . ." She slid into the bathroom and loitered behind the door, watching Ugo impassively wheeling forward the cart of dishes.

The instant he reached the balcony and had his back to her, Megan hurried out and away to the hall door, hearing 'Tessa directing, "Just set the covers, Ugo; Miss Royce has not arrived. Don't uncover the dishes; we'll serve ourselves."

"Sì, Contessa . . ."

Stepping down the side staircase as silently as possible, Megan slithered into the deserted entrance hall and threw the mail on the foyer table. She lingered briefly, to arrange letters and papers as if at random—and behind her a voice spoke harshly, "What are you about, Miss Royce?"

"I took the mail from the postman," she said, continuing to flip through the pile. "I hoped for a letter from my uncle, but there's nothing for me today." she turned to smile innocently at 'Renzo. "Shall I take your mother's mail?"

"Certainly not! That is a servant's duty!" He strode forward and nervously shuffled everything together again. "I fail to understand why the mail should have been handed to you in the first place. It is well known that Ugo is to receive the post and bring it to me at once."

"To *you*?"

"Well, well," he said impatiently, "to the estate office, if you prefer. There are affairs of business to be handled; those take precedence."

"Of course," she said sweetly, making no move to leave, "but since you're here, perhaps you'd sort out your mother's letters?" She was quite aware it was dangerous to needle 'Renzo, but she couldn't resist. She turned to look at the view from the entrance door, so that he would have a chance to inspect the mail. "It's such a lovely day—should I persuade your mother to come on the water with me?"

"That would be a kind thought, Miss Royce." 'Renzo was restored to good humor; he extended the letters. "I'm sure Mama would enjoy it." As she started up the staircase, he added, "Miss Royce, you will not misunderstand if I ask that in the future you do not receive the Vellanti postbag? I know you meant only to be helpful, but this is Ugo's responsibility, and we have our routine. If I had not happened to be at hand," he shrugged gracefully, "you would have left everything where it might not have been discovered for hours."

"Yes, of course, Prince di Frecchia—it was extremely thoughtless of me. Somehow you've all made me feel—part of the family rather than a guest." She looked down at him squarely. "But I truly don't mean to interfere with *anything* at Vellanti."

His eyes sharpened involuntarily, but he was still smiling. "Oh, we make too much of this; it is no tragedy, after all! Enjoy your luncheon, Miss Royce."

"You will have to buy stamps, Megan," the Contessa said later. "Customarily, Ugo collects everything left on the hall table and arranges the postage."

Megan tucked the half-dozen letters in the bottom of her tote bag. "Why not come with me? I told Lorenzo I meant to suggest it, and he thought it was a good idea."

"I think we won't chance it," the Contessa said slowly. "I suspect someone would turn up to accompany us, and there would be some reason why we should not land anywhere. No, we must hope you'll be unsuspected and allowed to go alone. I even think that we should broadcast that I do not go with you."

Tessa frowned thoughtfully. "And to make all safer—you tell everyone you are going only to Isola and will be back for tea. Head away from the nearest towns—refuel at Isola if needed. Then go on to Menaggio. Once you round the point at Isola, it will be a while before it's realized you may have gone further—but I think that little while may be long enough for you to reach Menaggio before the big launch could overtake you." She looked somberly at Megan. "I do not like any of this; you are far too young."

"All the healthier to take care of you."

"I should never have brought you, but how could I *dream* . . ."

"Yes. Well, nefarious plots are not the first thing one anticipates, but once they come to mind, self-preservation is the first law of nature," Megan said. "If my ancestors had guts—and they did—I've got 'em too." She stood up with decision.

"From now on, I can be a planned inconvenience, because nobody knows we've got the drop on them. Oh, yes, I know it's dangerous," Megan said quietly, as the Contessa started to speak. "But they'll do almost anything to avoid harming *me*. I'm not expendable, as they thought. I'm a penniless orphan, yes—but I'm receiving regular letters from friends, so I can't just disappear. I'll bet *that* was a blow! The alternative is two bodies instead of one—two fatal accidents take a deal of explaining, 'Tessa."

After a moment, the Contessa asked, "Who are 'they,' Megan?"

"I wish I knew," Megan said soberly, "and maybe it's only 'he,' but I think we should assume the worst and plan accordingly. This is how I see it: as of now, you go nowhere and do nothing until I've done it first. Don't even eat anything unless it's also been served to me. I've already sprung the major trap by pure chance. At this moment, the one safe place in Vellanti is the boathouse: a trap was tried there, and it failed; it can't be repeated.

"By the same token," Megan went on slowly, "they can't risk my springing another one. They'll watch me like hawks; any time I'm likely to gum the works, I'll be deflected. Then we'll know what to avoid. One thing; we mustn't be caught together—I go first, and you follow only when I've proved it safe."

The Contessa's eyes filled with tears. "There have been other attempts," she stated. "You know something I do not. Oh, Megan—my dear, you must leave at once; I cannot allow you to risk your life— and that is what you will be doing if you stay. You are American; you don't know; you can't understand . . ."

"No, I can't understand—but I can accept the existence of pure evil, even if I never expected to meet it face to face. I'd better tell you: I've already written a detailed exposition of the situation to date, and I mailed it to Uncle Joe this morning in Cernobbia," Megan said steadily. "I shall somehow make this fact public at dinner tonight. It may result in putting the boat out of use—but it will also cause everyone to think furiously!

"The instant Uncle Joe gets the letter, he will *do* something—and 'Renzo is well aware of it. It will take about four days to reach New York, but if anything happened to me, there'd be hell to pay. If anything happens to you—well, Miss Royce has been ill; she is the fanciful, hysterical type . . ." Megan shrugged. "So *I'm* safe—and we concentrate on *you,* because if you're still here five days from now, they'll find their hands completely tied!" She laughed heartily. "Wait till I tell you . . ."

Rapidly she outlined: "We can't tell the Zhondeks the phone doesn't work—they'll either get it fixed or hire a car to drive out here! We can't tell the Embassy doctor we're not at home—if an accident is about to happen! There's no way to prevent our joining the Zhondeks in their car, for a jaunt to Bologna. But the best of all," Megan chortled, "d'you realize they haven't the least idea that any of this is about to occur!" She extended a persuasive hand to the Contessa.

"*Andiamo* . . . Up the Braves, and Forward the Buffs! Ring for the servants to remove the dishes, come downstairs with me, and ring for servants to place a lounge chair on the terrace. Let us be overheard: my inviting you to a boat ride and your refusal." She eyed the Contessa thoughtfully and had a wily idea. "Say that you aren't sure whether you've caught a cold or ate something that disagreed with you," she suggested. "That will explain your anxious face—because the vital thing is—*no one must realize you know, 'Tessa!*"

"You are right as always, my dear. I shall have a slight headache . . ."

"Due to an upset tummy."

The Contessa stood up. "I wonder why you insist on that?"

"Because *I* brought you a basket of fresh figs,"

Megan said glibly, "and there's nothing like a good red herring is there?"

"All Italians are born actors," Megan thought, observing the Contessa's interpretation of her role. Wanly, Mrs. Waldron requested *un digestif* while the footman was deftly removing the luncheon dishes. Feebly, she was persuaded to totter down the main staircase in full view of half the castle servants. She sadly refused Megan's invitation for a boat ride. Within five minutes it was known that la Contessa was not feeling herself—because the whole scene was played in Italian, to be certain no one missed a word.

Megan played right along, exhibiting disappointment followed by exquisite tact in removing herself so 'Tessa might rest. She retreated on a note of regret and anxiety. "Elise, another two aspirins at four, but if she is asleep, do not wake her."

A major production from start to finish! 'Renzo came bustling out to the terrace. "What is this, Mama? You are not feeling well? Elise, send for Dr. Silvio at once!"

"No, no, it is only that I ate too many of Megan's fresh figs—say nothing, 'Renzo! She meant only to please me, and I was piggish . . ."

Quietly, Megan faded away from the scene on the terrace, clutching the tote bag with 'Tessa's letters. The foyer was empty; the great doors were open to the sun. The golf cart stood in its usual spot, to one side and half hidden by shrubbery, waiting to transport its mistress down the hill. Swiftly, Megan hopped into the seat and pressed the starting button. With luck, she would reach the boathouse before anyone even knew she was gone.

She was halfway down the curving drive when she realized it was not Megan Royce, but the golf cart brakes that were gone.

Behind her, a chorus of frantic male yells arose. From the corner of her eye she could see Ugo and Cesare dashing wildly across the great lawn to intercept her. Even as she hurtled uncontrollably forward, her mind was coldly analytical: she could save herself at any moment by springing out to a patch of grass—why not give them a run for their money? One firm hand controlled the steering lever, the other secured the tote bag containing those so dangerous letters of 'Tessa's. There was a stretch of turf beyond Casa Piccola; that was where she'd jump.

"Mees, *Mees!*" Ugo's voice was a scream. "Stop, *Stop!*" Megan looked over her shoulder casually, waved a hand and smiled, as 'Renzo dashed out to the castle steps, clasping his hands in horror before trotting down to the driveway. Cesare was wasting no breath, but streaking on a well-planned course likely to catch her.

Megan touched the gas pedal and bounded forward, but even so, he nearly made it. "*Per Dio, jump!*" he panted, his hand sliding futilely from the back of the cart. "Megan, there are no brakes . . ." Occupied in selecting the Spot, she wasn't sure whether he'd used her first name or was merely saying "Mees."

"Dear Lord, let me remember how to do a rolling fall!" she prayed silently. Deliberately, she twisted the steering lever to direct the cart on an unobstructed course and sprang for the turf—tucking her head between her arms, letting her body go limp until it rolled to a stop at the bottom of the gradient . . .

CHAPTER NINE

She lay breathless for a moment, slowly aware of
small discomforts: a tiny throb beneath her left shoulder blade where she must have whammed against a
stone—a stinging sensation on her right arm that was
probably a long scrape from the first slithering contact with the grass. There was a minor strangulation
about her wrist that was the tote bag containing
'Tessa's letters. Instinctively, her hand curled even
more firmly about the straps, and she opened her
eyes—to stare up at Cesare's ashen face.

He dropped down on one knee, grasping her shoulders, but so out of breath that Megan got in first. "I'm
so sorry—but I'm still not dead, Prince Cesare . . ."

"No thanks to you," he said hoarsely, releasing her
so suddenly that she fell back on the grass once more.
"You were present, I believe," he stood up, grim-
jawed, "when I stated that *no* equipment was to be
used until Ugo approved?" Looming over her, straight-
ening jacket and shirt cuffs, Cesare looked nine feet
tall—and Ugo appeared at his side, equally tall,
silent and minatory.

Megan wondered, "Was that the second attempt
today? They must be getting desperate!" She rolled
over and up to her feet. "Indeed I was present—but
I confess I'd no idea everything at Vellanti was in

142

such critical shape, Prince Cesare. We used the golf cart only two days ago—and *now* the brakes have given way?"

Ugo broke into an impassioned guttural mutter that was beyond her, but Cesare nodded, "No one blames you, Ugo."

"Mees might have been killed," Ugo growled stolidly.

"Yes—and entirely her own fault." There was a pregnant pause. "Ugo, see whether the cart can be salvaged. I will take Miss Royce—where were you going?"

"To the boathouse," Megan said clearly. "Ugo approved the runabout yesterday; I used it this morning. It runs *beautifully*, Ugo!" He ducked his head ungraciously as always, and started away. "I tried to persuade your mother to come with me, but she didn't feel up to it, so I left her to rest," Megan shrugged. "I meant to run up to Isola for sun and fresh air." She turned to the path—and found herself neatly caught between Cesare's glowering face behind her, and 'Renzo hastily approaching ahead. "A perfect panzer movement," Megan thought. "Cannon to right of me, cannon to left of me, cannon in front of me . . . into the valley of Death walked the six hundred . . ."

Megan reached the path, then hesitated, glancing at her watch, "I guess it's too late for a ride, now."

"Yes, Miss Royce, it is," Cesare assured her evenly, catching her elbow in steely fingers. "You have had an unpleasant experience; reaction will emerge shortly. I will conduct you to Casa Piccola, and if you should feel unable to join us for dinner, we will quite understand."

"Miss Royce . . . Cesare, what happened?" 'Renzo asked anxiously, facing them at the steps.

"Miss Royce most foolishly attempted to use Mama's golf cart before Ugo had set the brakes in order. There is just so much time in a day, after all! Ugo cannot be expected to work miracles. Perhaps if he had not spent yesterday in preparing the boat for our guest's amusement, there might have been time to check the cart used by the hostess at Vellanti—but Miss Royce is American and seems not to understand this. However, there is no harm done."

"Not to me, but I expect the cart is a total loss. You must allow me to replace it . . ."

"Nonsense!" 'Renzo frowned, running a hand over her arm as if to assure himself no bones were broken. "Cesare, I *insist* we send for Dr. Silvio! Here is Mama lying on the terrace with some sort of gastric trouble, and now our guest may be suffering from shock, concussion, who knows what?" He broke into Italian, but his words were sufficiently clear that Megan knew she was intended to understand. "How you can have allowed Vellanti to go to rack and ruin in this fashion, Cesare!"

"Mama is *ill*?"

"A slight headache," Megan said soothingly, "probably from overeating the figs I brought her—you know how she loves them."

"Yes, indeed! You know Mama and figs, Cesare. What a kind thought, Miss Royce . . ."

"I cannot agree; it appears to me Miss Royce rarely thinks at all." Cesare's voice was a snarl. "In the course of only one day, she appears to have ruined both Mama's digestion and the golf cart."

"Tchk, Cesare, you forget yourself. Why, Miss Royce might have broken her neck!"

144

"An admirable solution, Prince di Frecchia," Megan said smoothly, as Cesare whirled furiously on his brother, "but I'm bound to add, I think it'd be terribly awkward for everyone." Shaking off 'Renzo's hand, she went up the steps and looked down at them. "You will say *nothing* of this accident to your mother," she stated. Their faces stared at her blankly.

"It is, as you pointed out, Prince Cesare, entirely my own fault—and would not have occurred if the Contessa had been with me," Megan purred innocently, "for then Ugo would have been at hand to prevent it. This happened only because I left unobtrusively and was too lazy to walk. And everybody was attending to her comfort, naturally.

"But it would not be pleasant for 'Tessa to hear of this. As you've both so often told me, she isn't young. Inevitably, she'll imagine it might have been she in the cart . . ." Someone—was it 'Renzo or Cesare?—sucked in his breath involuntarily, but Megan had abandoned prudence in favor of bitchery. She had decided to let 'em sweat, to let 'em wonder how much she knew and how dangerous she might be! Megan meant to get the Contessa away from Vellanti this very night, somehow—and until then, she'd damn well enjoy needling.

"Of course, Ugo would have protected the Contessa," she said, "but on top of that accident in the boathouse, she's bound to worry. So you will arrange to shut the servants' mouths and laugh the whole thing off as a mere nothing. If you like, say it was my inexpert handling." She shrugged. "I'll back any story you like, but your mother is not to be distressed further; *is that clear?*"

"Entirely—and it is like you to think first of Mama," 'Renzo approved. "Ah well," he clapped

Cesare's shoulder happily, "all's well that ends well, eh? Miss Royce will rest here, Ugo will dispatch a light dinner, and Anna Maria will make her comfortable. Come, Cesare, we must not detain Miss Royce longer."

Cesare shook off his brother's urgent fingers, staring impassively at Megan. "Where did you produce these figs that upset Mama so badly?" he inquired softly.

Click! Megan turned away, letting her shoulders droop wearily, striving desperately for the right answer. "Figs?" she murmured vaguely. "Oh, *figs!* I'm sorry, I *am* beginning to feel the reaction as you prophesied."

Before her, Anna Maria was throwing open the door, trotting forward to support Megan soothingly. "Mees, come upstairs at once . . ."

"The figs, Miss Royce?" Cesare's voice rolled like thunder, stiffening Megan's backbone at once. Hah, he expected to hear of mushrooms?

"Why, I got them from the usual man—I don't know his name. He has a mustache and a red bandanna, and he puts in at all the landings," she said vaguely. "I expect you know him; I often buy oranges —but today was the first time he had fresh figs, so I bought the whole basket for 'Tessa."

"This transaction took place on the water?" At Megan's indifferent nod, he asked, "Where else did you go, Miss Royce?"

He'd been right that reaction would set in speedily; every inch of Megan's body ached cruelly as she leaned against Anna Maria and stepped into the foyer. "Where did I go?" she echoed, bracing herself against the iron grille and losing her temper completely. "If

146

you must know—although I can't see it's any of your business—I had a rendezvous with my lover."

The effect was all she could have wished. Cesare stepped back as if she'd struck him—and 'Renzo's eyebrows flew up to his receding hairline. "*Lover?*" he squeaked incredulously. "What is this; you have a lover at Vellanti? *Who is he?*"

Megan took a firm grip on the front door. "Why, Ugo, of course—who else?" She smiled sweetly and shut the heavy grille in their faces.

By sheer willpower, Megan got up to the bedroom —to call Elise on the estate phone, to say, "*Ne regardez pas quoiqu'on dit!* Tell the Contessa I am perfectly all right, that everything is going according to plan, and that I will see her at dinner."

"*Oui*—but what happens, Ma'mselle?" The maid's voice was lowered. "*J'ai peur . . .*"

Holding the phone, Megan could see the di Frecchia men walking around the curving driveway—Ugo striding up from the boathouse. Would anyone else monitor the estate phone? She must chance it! "Elise, *écoutez vif*: tonight I take Madame away for safety. You will make ready warm clothing to dress her after dinner—a fur coat, warm gloves, and a thick scarf for her head. Place her important papers and keys in a handbag—*mais prend garde!* All must seem as usual, yet ready *à l'instant! D'accord?*"

"*Sans doute! A bientôt . . .*"

For two hours, Megan applied herself to restoring her body. A soaking hot bath, one stiff shot of brandy, and a superb massage from Anna Maria did marvels —but even as Megan relaxed drowsily beneath the skillful stroking fingers, she was aware of unwonted silence. "Why so quiet?"

147

"I do not wish to disturb Mees by foolish chatter," the girl said smoothly, but her covert glance was unexpectedly shrewd as she turned for the massage cream.

"She knows something," Megan thought. "Is she involved? Could there be an estate plot—everyone working to get rid of Mama so Cesare inherits? Oh, *no*! That's too fantastic!" Megan strove to reassure herself—but she'd long realized the remarkable unity among the workers, and she had termed it a "fierce loyalty" to Prince Cesare. How fierce might that loyalty be?

'Tessa was right: Megan had no standards by which to judge expectable actions by Italian peasants. The concept of a hundred families smilingly banded together to murder an elderly woman for her son's benefit was incredible—but Vellanti was feudal; one mustn't forget that! Heaven knows, Cesare had told her often enough.

There was a third possibility Megan hadn't thought of before, and it was by far the most dangerous— if everyone at Vellanti was in the know, it made no difference whether or not 'Renzo were actively plotting with his brother. He stood to gain equally, and there'd be no help from him—in fact, it was a situation tailor-made for the pipsqueak. Officially, he had to know nothing, while someone pulled his chestnuts from the fire!

Still, if this were the wellspring of murder, Megan couldn't take 'Tessa away; she'd only lead both of them to death. In fact, that was exactly what a would-be murderer would find most desirable: to catch two birds with one stone, with Megan tagged as the patsy and blamed for causing the Contessa's death through inexpertise.

Megan would have to dig out what Anna Maria knew, and if it indicated a major plot, Megan must leave alone under cover of darkness tonight, try for Cernobbia, and telephone for help first thing tomorrow morning. The Contessa should be safe in her barricaded suite until Megan could return, and Elise, at least, was trustworthy.

Megan lay on her back with her eyes closed while Anna Maria worked down one arm. "How is Maria's baby? Talk to me, or I'll fall asleep."

"A few hours' nap would be best, Mees."

"There isn't time; I have to dress for dinner."

The stroking hands trembled uncontrollably for an instant, then steadied to the rhythm again. "But no, Mees, it is arranged: dinner will be brought here. I keep hot and serve when and where you like. Please, Mees, do not think of going to Casa Grande; it is too tiring for you tonight," Anna Maria babbled pleadingly. "I *like* to serve you, Mees."

"Thank you, but I must dine with the Contessa."

"*No!*" Anna Maria shrank back, pressing a hand to her mouth and staring wildly at Megan.

"Why not?" Megan asked, gently, but the girl only shook her head and muttered, "*Perdono*, Mees, I speak without thinking. The other arm, if you please."

"No, you aren't thinking, Anna Maria. If I do not appear, the Contessa will imagine that I am lying in pieces! Well, I am not . . ."

"*Press' a poco!*"

"No, not even almost in pieces, only a few bruises —but unless she sees for herself, she will worry. So, you will find me the dinner dress with long sleeves to hide the scratch, and I shall go at the usual time, to reassure her."

"I go with you, then. Turn for the back, please."

149

"Why? I can walk perfectly well." The maid's face was stubborn, and Megan propped herself on one elbow. "Why must you go with me, Anna Maria—you have a reason," she insisted. "Tell me!"

"*Io ho spavento . . . timo . . .*" The girl's face crumpled, she made a despairing gesture of her hand. "I do not know what I fear; I was never afraid before, nor anyone at Vellanti—but now, all is different. Oh, Mees, what is it that happens?" Anna Maria was half crying, wringing her hands in anguish. "These accidents, never do we have accidents at Vellanti! Now, who knows what occurs next, or where? Roberto cuts his leg with the scythe—Gian Carlo's promised bride runs away to Rome; she wants to be an actress . . . even Maria," she continued tremulously, "the new baby does not thrive. I do not like to tell you, Mees, but now . . . It is as though there were a curse on Vellanti."

"I see." Megan flopped onto her tummy and automatically the massage resumed. "Everything has happened since *I* arrived. Is it thought that perhaps I brought the curse to Vellanti?" she asked after a while.

"We are not so superstitious, Mees. It is recalled that the most dangerous accident occurs to you—and known that *il Cardinale* himself has blessed and embraced you as a member of the family—but now, there is another accident, and *to you,* Mees . . . and I am practical; I ask myself: Who . . ." her voice quivered and died away.

"Who, at Vellanti, wishes to kill me?" Megan finished placidly, ignoring the whispered, "*Sì . . .*" She turned her head on her crossed arms and smiled. "Well, I will tell you, Anna Maria: *no one.* Today, I am embarrassed at my stupidity! Prince Cesare

150

asked that I do not use any equipment until it has been checked. Ugo knew the cart had no brakes; it was not anticipated that I would forget Prince Cesare's request, and instantly both Ugo and the Prince came to my rescue. That's all."

"Why was the cart left in its usual place?" Anna Maria asked. "If Ugo has time to discover the brakes do not work, he has time to remove the cart. It takes no more than a minute to wheel it around to the garage, after all. At Vellanti, the only rule is complete safety for *people*; this you do not know, Mees, but *il Principe* never forgives *any* mistake or disobedience if it concerns someone's safety. And of all people at Vellanti, Ugo knows the rule from his childhood," Anna Maria finished, tossing a cover over Megan and stepping back to wipe her hands on a towel. "And *now,* suddenly, Ugo is careless?"

"Damn; she's far too smart!" Megan thought anxiously. "I must deflect her before she reaches the end: Contessa . . ." "There has to be a first time for anything," she said casually, aloud. "What time is it—nearly six? Should I have a quick shower to remove the cream, or should I let it absorb?"

"You should go to bed and sleep," Anna Maria returned austerely, "but if you will not, you will not, and I say no more." She rapidly folded the massage table and removed the tray of creams and towels as Megan went to wash her hands and face. In comparative silence, she assisted Megan into clothes and left her to accomplish makeup and hairdo, taking away the massage equipment. She returned just as Megan was wondering what to do with 'Tessa's letters: stuff them into her evening purse—or would it perhaps be better to burn them? She must run absolutely no risks of search and discovery, even if the Contessa had to write them over again . . . because there was always the silent watcher in the night, who might go through Megan's room while she was at dinner.

Anna Maria seemed oblivious of the envelopes in Megan's hand. She walked into the bedroom with determination and stood firm. "It is not you, but la Contessa who is threatened," she stated, with dignity. "And you protect her. There is something more; Elena hints to me—I do not ask to know, but if you take care of la Contessa, I take care of you." She looked squarely at Megan. "So, too, will all of Vellanti, Mees."

Megan hesitated, turning to the dressing table and thinking furiously. Could she trust this girl? But if there were a large-scale plot, Elena would never have let her see the amanitas, and Anna Maria would never have mentioned the oddity of the accidents. "Would you help la Contessa, even if it meant—not helping Prince Cesare?" she asked quietly.

"I cannot *believe* it is so," the girl whispered after a moment, "yet if it is . . . Vellanti will expect me to aid her." She looked pleadingly at Megan. "I rather not know anything—but I do whatever you say helps la Contessa."

"It's not so desperate." Megan smiled reassuringly. "Only, there have been difficulties with the mail. Do you think you could take some letters to a post box without anyone seeing?"

"But that is simple, Mees . . ."

"How will you do it?"

"I tell Luigi I like to ride with him to Cernobbia, to buy the movie magazine." Anna Maria grinned wickedly. "He is so proud of the Vespa, so tonight I go—and he will be too pleased to notice what I do!"

Megan extended the letters. "The only task is to mail these without anyone knowing . . . There must even be a reason if Luigi sees you placing something in a post box, you understand?"

The maid nodded and thrust the letters into the deep pocket of the uniform beneath her cloak. "Have no fear, Mees. If you are ready, I walk up with you —then I find Luigi. It takes an hour for us to go and return, but"—she looked sternly at Megan—"you wait! I come back to bring you home. *Convenuto?*"

"Yes, agreed!"

The Contessa was resplendent as usual, but with sunken, shadowed eyes. There was a major *bouleversement* at Megan's entrance. "You should not have attempted . . . All was arranged for rest . . . You are certain you feel well enough?"

"Of course," Megan pretended surprise. "There's not a thing wrong with me; I had a tumble on the grass, in all. 'Tessa, how are *you*? Figs! Next time I shall dole them out!"

"Are you really all right, Megan?"

"See for yourself." Gaily she walked back and forth, à la mannequin and drew a smile from the Contessa. "Good as new!"

"Better," 'Renzo approved. "Ah, if only they had *you* to model at those dreary society balls, Miss Royce!"

Cesare's face was inscrutable. Suddenly he drained his martini and grinned sardonically. "One more turn, Miss Royce, *por l'amore di Dio!*" he begged, earnestly—and at the lightening in the Contessa's expression, Megan gave it everything. She slung forward, held out a fold of the skirt disdainfully, and improvised a sales talk in flat, totally uninterested Brooklynese.

For a moment, everyone looked blank; then 'Tessa snorted gently and broke into laughter. Cesare's face was intent, willing but not entirely *with* it, until Megan ended: "This exclusive model comes in all sizes and a full range of fashion colors, for only eight ninety-five, available only at S. Klein." Whether or not Cesare had ever heard of Klein's he got the gist and laughed heartily.

'Renzo's face was smiling politely—but still blank . . .

For the first time, both men joined the Contessa and Megan after dinner and did *not* excuse themselves. Conversation hobbled along, principally from 'Renzo, but even he was not in form this evening. A faint miasma of weariness hung over the room, and Megan realized that 'Tessa was growing tired and nervous, wanting to be alone to plan. When Ugo announced that Anna Maria was ready to walk back to Casa Piccola with Mees, D day had arrived.

There was an instant bustle of relief, and 'Renzo sprang to his feet. "Thank you, Ugo, Miss Royce will be ready at once—I'm sure you're longing for bed . . . should not have made the effort to join us, delightful as it is to have you with us, adding so much . . ."

Cesare, standing also, said, "You are for bed, too, Mama? Eleven o'clock! Ugo, send for Elise . . ."

The Contessa's dark eyes receded into shadows again, staring silently at Megan.

"Why bother Elise? I'll take 'Tessa to her room. I left my scarf at lunchtime; I might as well get it now. Ugo, tell Anna Maria to wait a minute, please." She had the Contessa nearly to the stairs before 'Renzo strode forward nervously.

"This is absurd! Ugo, conduct Mama to her suite and fetch Miss Royce's scarf."

Megan's hand tightened, bracing the trembling

elbow. "But I should like to walk up with your mother and get my scarf," she said. "Have you some —objection, Prince di Frecchia?"

There was a long pause, as though a breath were being collectively held. From the staircase, Megan could see the three men standing motionless: Ugo, stolidly eyeing the floor . . . Cesare, saturnine and impassive, in the doorway to the salon . . . Prince di Frecchia, flushing scarlet with fury, on the brink of a scene . . . Ugo cleared his throat, muffled a cough, and muttered "*Pardone . . .*"

Prince di Frecchia's color subsided slowly. "You choose strange words, Miss Royce. The only 'objection' is that you have had an accident, should be in bed at this moment, and are proposing to do a servant's errand. I make allowances for American independence, but things are different here!"

"Women are not different *anywhere*, Prince di Frecchia. If you like to waste Ugo's energy by sending him to retrieve my scarf—which is really not too heavy for me to carry—by all means do so. I shall still accompany your mother to her suite, where we will chat until she is ready for sleep."

"You force me to say that I *forbid* you to disturb Mama."

"You force *me* to remind you that, like myself, you are only a guest at Vellanti." Megan's fingers impelled 'Tessa onward and upward.

"Miss Royce"—Cesare's deep voice rolled across the foyer—"my brother puts it badly—but we are concerned that both you and Mama shall have rest. Please, not too long a chat?"

"Of course not! Goodnight." Megan bowed to the Contessa. "We had such a delicious dinner, we should thank Elena," she said at random.

"Yes, that would be a kind thought. Ugo, see to it."
But in the suite she nearly collapsed. "They know!"
she whispered, clutching Megan's hands frantically.
"Oh, my dear, you must leave!"

"Not without you." Megan shook her head calmly.
"And they do not *know*, they only suspect there is
something to be known. Now we must arrange very
quickly, they will watch how long I stay. Elise, you
must help . . ."

"First we will have a *fine*, Elise," the Contessa said
firmly. "One for yourself, too. One always thinks better with brandy." She looked at Megan. "My letters?"

"Mailed this evening by Anna Maria, and no one
is the wiser. Now." She took the tiny brandy snifter
absently, "listen well:

"I shall go back and apparently to bed. You will
dress in warm, dark clothing, walking shoes, and a
fur coat—it will be cold on the water. Elise, at precisely five minutes to one, you must reconnoiter; if
there should be anyone in the hall watching the suite,
you must *somehow* deflect them while the Contessa
slips out and down the side stairs. *Compris?*"

"*Mais oui, je fais le Grand Guignol, je vous assure!
Ah, les punaises!*"

"Yes, they're lice but we haven't time to discuss
them now. 'Tessa, the instant Elise clears the way,
you come quickly to unlatch the side door—do not
open it, just unlatch it and stand in the hall until I
see that all is clear outside."

"Then what?"

Megan shrugged. "We slither down to the boathouse on our bellies like snakes, if necessary. We get
into a boat, and we vamoose. With luck we reach
Como; without, we hit Cernobbia where 'At Your

Service' Montoro will assist us. Either way, we are *gone*, and between Elise and Anna Maria this should not be discovered until noon tomorrow. The only dangerous bit is getting you down to the boat unobserved." Megan finished her brandy and stood up. "Elise, get me a scarf no one will recognize."

The Contessa's dark eyes were unfathomable, looking at Megan over the liqueur glass. Suddenly, she lifted it in the gesture of a toast, drained it, and sent it crashing over her shoulder, to splinter against the fireplace. "You have reached the *ne plus ultra*," she said, and chuckled at Megan's startled face. "I half think you may pull it off, my dear."

"I shall. His Eminence gave me a special blessing and said it was for taking care of you."

"Massimo is very wise."

"God is even wiser," Megan said dryly, "and I was raised to think He's always ready to back good against evil. I shall see you at one . . ."

Megan came leisurely down the grand staircase, twirling the scarf over her fingers, and instantly both di Frecchias emerged from the salon, prepared to escort her. "Where is Anna Maria?" She glanced about vaguely, stuffing the scarf into the pocket of her evening coat.

"Oh, there is no need for her, Miss Royce, when we are both here, as you see. Ugo," 'Renzo ordered, completely restored to good humor, "tell the girl she is not needed."

"But she *is* needed," Megan contradicted gently. "Ugo, tell her I'm ready, please." Placidly, she sat down on the hall bench while the man went through the service door. "If anyone is unnecessary," she remarked, "it is yourself—and Prince Cesare."

"I beg your pardon, I—think I cannot have understood you . . ."

"Nor I, you," she said. "You speak constantly of 'servant duties,' Prince di Frecchia, and imply very strongly that an American knows nothing of servant management. No doubt you are right; in America we have employees rather than servants, but the top executive never fails to recognize effort. Anna Maria has voluntarily given up her off-duty hours this evening in order to help me do what gives me pleasure. She is not now to be told she is unnecessary and must walk home alone in the night, merely because Prince di Frecchia fancies an evening stroll."

"A masterly exposition of the American viewpoint, Miss Royce," Cesare remarked. "Based on Dr. Innisperg?"

"No, I figured it out all by myself," Megan said sweetly, while 'Renzo was controlling himself with main force. "Ah, here is Anna Maria," she said, as the girl followed Ugo into the foyer and bobbed respectfully to the two men. "Sorry to be so long, Anna Maria. The door, if you please, Ugo?" Megan rose calmly, drifting forward with a nod and a smile. "Goodnight, again . . ."

"I shall come with you, even if not required, Miss Royce," Cesare said, and picked up the heavy lantern. "It is true there are no wolves nor lions at Vellanti, and I humbly confess I attend you merely because *I* fancy a stroll—but you will not condemn me to walk alone, even so? Ah, no," he said dramatically, "you have too tender a heart!"

"What nonsense you babble, Cesare! Very well," 'Renzo said. He strode forward tight-lipped and snatched a second lantern. "We will *all* go, since this suits our guest's notions of proper conduct."

158

Megan slid her hand through the maid's arm and could feel it trembling; but with deliverance in view, she was not minded to concede an inch. Academically, she wondered what particular tiny disaster had been planned for this evening. Part way along the path she turned her ankle, very slightly and carefully, but requiring a masculine arm to steady her. She chose 'Renzo and leaned her full weight against him, so that it required all his attention to keep her aloft. Behind her, Cesare politely assisted the maid to negotiate the slopes and steps—but at least there was no possibility of a dual fatality, to include Anna Maria.

The girl was white-faced by the time she'd closed the iron entrance grille and faced Megan's query, "The letters?"

"Posted in Cernobbia, and Luigi did not see. Oh, Mees—I am afraid for you! His face, did you see? Like the days of the Underground before someone was to be killed."

"Whose face—and how would you know anything about the Underground? You weren't even born."

"Ugo, Mees—and it is what the older people tell us, that he looks so . . ."

"I see." That made sense. Megan wondered why she hadn't thought of it before. Ugo, who could go anywhere and everywhere, unquestioned by day or by night—and who was devoted to Prince di Frecchia. "Are you afraid of Ugo?"

"Yes and no—he is so stern and silent, but he would never harm anyone from Vellanti."

"Then you will help me a bit more? I shall explain *nothing*, so you will know only—that I change my clothes, go to the boathouse and finally to the castle . . . but I must not be seen, I cannot use a lantern, and I do not know the paths."

"I come with you, Mees," Anna Maria whispered after a moment.

"Good—but there's not much time. Can you find dark clothes? I can dress myself . . ."

Swiftly, she found black slacks and shirt, dark jacket and gloves, tennis shoes—navy would pass for black in the night. Thank heavens her coat was black seal, five years old but still warm. Into the buttoned jacket pockets went her passport, money, names and addresses, boathouse keys, cigarettes—and a plentiful supply of matches.

Moving back and forth, she tried to give the impression of preparing for bed to any watching eyes. Were there any? She restrained the impulse to peek. Fifteen minutes later she was dressed: it took five minutes to restudy the plans—she mustn't forget anything or leave any clue. *Uncle Joe's letter!* She retrieved it and Dr. Innisperg's from her evening purse and with steady fingers burned them both, flushing the ashes down the toilet. For good measure, she pulled out all her traveling cases and searched them; she had no way to tell if the disappearance of the diamond clip had been discovered, but at least nothing new had been added.

Shortly before midnight, Megan lowered the lights and peeked out. The watcher was in place—less obvious than last night, but still the flicker of lantern light wasn't quite hidden by the shrubbery. Was it Ugo? What would happen if she boldly went out the front entrance and accosted him, saying she fancied a breath of air before bed? It was a lovely thought, Megan grinned wickedly—but of course it was *not* practical.

Anna Maria came softly into the room. "I am ready,

Mees, and I have brought a cloak for you, to hide the head." She took one glance at Megan's alert stance and paled. "Someone watches?"

"Yes; he was there last night, too. So now we pretend: do exactly what you would do if I were climbing into bed—and say 'goodnight' very clearly at the window, so it may be heard . . ."

"Sì," the girl went quickly through the motions of closing up for the night, while Megan threw the cloak about herself and adjusted the hood to shadow her face. Exactly as Anna Maria opened the window and said clearly, "Buon' sònno, Mees." Megan turned out the bedlamp and said, "Grazie, a domani." She went out to the landing, while the maid closed the bedroom door.

"No more conversation; you lead and I follow," Megan whispered. "But do exactly what you always do."

They went down the stairs, barred the door, turned off the outside entrance lights and the foyer chandelier, and moved to the kitchen—and Anna Maria hesitated, for the first time scared. "I forget, I have no key. Always we bar this door from inside."

Megan stood in the shadows of the service door and debated: if they locked, Anna Maria was left in the chill—if they snecked the latch for re-entry, there was the chance someone would discover the open door, investigate and raise the alarm. "If you couldn't get back into Casa Piccola, where would you go?"

"No place," the girl shrugged helplessly. "It is nearly five miles up and across the fields to my father's house . . ."

Megan decided to chance it. She snecked the latch and gestured, whispering. "Let's go . . ."

CHAPTER TEN

She could never have hoped to accomplish this without Anna Maria, Megan realized as they stole down
across the slope. The girl knew every inch of Vellanti, and she led Megan unerringly over silent grass
away from the paths, until they could see the tiny
plaza before the boathouse.

Breathlessly, they stood together in the shadows of
the shrubbery, while Megan contemplated the open
expanses to be traversed.

The warning moon was just rising like a half-rotten
pumpkin behind the Bellagio point. It was not shed-
ding much light, but already enough to be able to
see motion, to distinguish dark from less dark. Damn
that moon. It was something she hadn't thought of—
it would be easier to lead 'Tessa down from the castle—but detection would also be easier. She could
feel the maid's hand trembling on her elbow.

Megan laid her hand firmly over Anna Maria's and
stood listening, but there was no sound in the soft
night air. "Now I shall leave you here," she whispered, her lips near the maid's ear, "and if anyone
comes, you must lure them away somehow!" With a
final squeeze of reassurance, Megan ran lightly across
to the boathouse, the key ready in her hand. She in-

serted the key, turned it, opened the door, then closed it softly behind her.

For a moment she stood again, adjusting to the total blackness, hearing the lapping of water against the berths, *listening* . . . and there was still only silence above and below. When her eyes were dark-adapted, Megan cautiously moved forward along the crosswalk to the runabout and dared to strike a match. To her relief, the boat was still there.

Until she'd doused the match, Megan hadn't realized her inner anxiety that the boat might have been removed. So far, so good. Her heart bounced with confidence as she pulled the boat toward her, neatly stashed her coat under the seat, and let herself down. Working forward, she braced herself against a bulkhead and stretched up to unlock the water door. Then she worked back until she could feel her way on to the crosswalk.

Now she deliberately rested in the coolness, hearing no sound within or without, but only the lapping of water and the infinitesimal slap-whap of the boats bobbing at rest. What more?

She would need maps, a flashlight, extra petrol, waterproof cushions and life jackets . . . Megan crawled on hands and knees until her head bumped against the wooden door to the map room. By lighting another match, carefully, shielded, she found the chart she wanted; she found a flashlight purely by feel and made sure it worked by switching it on *within* its drawer. Back again she went to the boat, crawling inch by inch and finally adding chart and torch to the hidden coat. Cushions and jackets presented no problem; these festooned the boathouse walls. Megan tossed a couple of each into the boat and sat down to concentrate. Where did they keep the gasoline? Megan crawled back to the map room and found nothing, but it was all taking more time than was wise. She opened the door to the visitor's berth, and squandered three matches (because she couldn't be seen in here), but there was no row of petrol cans. She found a set of oars and pulled them over the planking through the map room—and promptly connected in the dark with the door to the crosswalk, in a thunderous crash that brought her heart to her throat.

Megan collapsed over the oars and lay still, feeling tears in her eyes. After a while, she realized they were tears of fury and determination. So she wasn't a female James Bond, but she was still going to prevent the murder of a decent woman if it killed everybody else, dammit!

Eventually, she hoicked the oars along as softly as possible and got them into the boat; there was still the gasoline to find. The boats were automatically filled each day, so there had to be some. Where in hell was it? She worked her way to the farther end and found only a blank wall; crawling back she had the answer— a petrol pump, with a long hose.

It was padlocked—but before Megan realized this, she'd happily upended the hose and lost what gasoline it contained, dribbling it into the water before she reached the runabout.

So that was that—and it was possible the boat had been automatically refilled as usual. There should be enough to reach Cernobbia, anyway; she'd refilled in Como this morning, and she couldn't have used all of it getting back to Vellanti . . . and there were oars.

She stood up finally and went to the door, making certain the keys were buttoned into her jacket pocket and reconnoitering briefly. She saw no sign of Anna Maria . . . but up the hillside a lantern bobbed toward her. She darted across to the shrubbery, "Someone's coming!"

"The guard," Anna Maria nodded, grabbing Megan's hand and retreating as swiftly as they had come. Simultaneously, the watchman swung, whistling, down the farther path to the boathouse, where he carefully tested both doors and flashed the lantern along the outer walls. Megan caught her breath. Would he check the rear door of Casa Piccola? Anna Maria was evidently way ahead of her; she urgently tugged Megan back to the guest house, as the man turned their way.

But they'd made it, locked and barred the door, and reached the safe darkness of the foyer before the man reached Casa Piccola—to test the kitchen door and shine his lantern briefly across the kitchen floor. Then he was moving around to the front, again testing, shining his light through windows and across the terrace . . .

Listening keenly, Megan could hear no greeting, no interchange of words, yet the guard had gone directly past the spot of the hidden watcher. Had the watcher left, once Megan seemed abed? There was no time to reconnoiter; Anna Maria was already waiting by the back door. "He won't return for three hours," she said softly. "From here he goes to the main gate, around by the greenhouse and back, to rest in the Vellanti guard room for his supper. Come on."

It was harder going up this last stretch, but the castle was silent and darkened, except for dimmed hall lights. Megan softly turned the knob of the side door, and with a suppressed sigh of relief, the Contessa stepped out. Behind her, Elise made a gamin thumbs-up sign and quietly closed the door. Megan could hear a click of the lock. Anna Maria was still with them, luckily for Megan. Wordlessly, she took the Contessa's other arm and together the girls got the older woman down to the boathouse.

It seemed an endless walk, and Megan was shaking inside by the time she'd unlocked the boathouse again and got 'Tessa into the boat, but eventually it was done. Anna Maria was gone with a silent grip of Megan's hand, and the door was refastened.

Now Megan could push open the lake doors and pull them from the berth—it would not be possible to shut these doors behind them; they would just have to hope that no one would investigate the water side. In the dull glow of the waning moon, the Contessa took a deep breath and smiled at Megan, who settled down to rowing. It was harder than she'd expected, since the boat wasn't meant for rowing, but Megan had planned to pull them down to the next landing before starting the engine. Then if they were heard, it might seem only to belong to that property.

Shipping the oars, she crossed her fingers and started the engine. There was still fuel, but how much? There should be enough to get them out of sight around the point, at least. Finally, they dared to talk. "Did you have any incident?" Megan asked.

"Only Ugo, wanting to apologize again for the accident and tell me the cart is not badly damaged. He was alone, so Elise opened the hall door and allowed him to hear my voice from the bedroom. Now he believes that at twelve thirty, the Contessa was in bed, if not yet asleep."

Megan nodded. "Good." So Ugo might have been

166

the watcher, but what could he have wanted to ascertain? Only that both Megan and la Contessa were in bed—how would that fit? Megan abandoned speculation and concentrated on steering.

"What about you, Megan?"

"Anna Maria helped; she led me on the side paths, but I explained nothing, so she can only say we went to the boathouse late at night. That's all she knows, so she can't be confused by questioning. I took the Bellagio charts, so it will seem we were heading across the lake. The only thing, 'Tessa—I don't know how much gas we have, and the pump was locked."

"Let's hope for the best."

The best brought them only to the cove before the last point facing Cernobbia. The engine coughed miserably, and subsided, leaving them rocking gently in moonlit silence. " 'Tessa, you know the terrain: What's best? Shall I row along to the point . . . or make for the shore; it's about a mile either way, but then—is there a summerhouse or a cottage so we can get under cover? And I think we should abandon the boat and walk, if you can."

"I *can,* and there is the Laurenti boathouse around the point, so we shall leave the boat here and take the path directly across. Pull in anywhere you like . . ."

"I brought a flashlight; I think we dare use it now."

"Yes—and perhaps overturn the boat, so it seems we ran out of gasoline and hit a rock? We can hide the oars somewhere in the underbush . . ."

Megan laughed helplessly, bending to the oars again. "You missed your calling; definitely you were meant to be a lady spy!" It was a major effort, but eventually they heaved the boat over and poked it as far as possible into the current at the trifling cost of one wet foot for Megan. "It'll dry out as I walk," she said cheerfully. "I'll have to wear my coat—should I leave the cloak floating in the water?"

"By all means," the Contessa agreed cordially, "and if you can drag the oars by yourself for a little while— give me the torch; I'll find the path." She strode ahead, with Megan stumbling behind and suddenly conscious of alarming aches and bone-weariness. Every bruise throbbed like a wound. The going was slightly easier after they had thrust the oars into a thicket, but still Megan was alarmed, because the Contessa was now burning her own energy—and how much did she have? And it was still Megan's responsibility to protect the Contessa and to get help tomorrow. And they still must traverse five water miles to Cernobbia.

At last, the boathouse loomed directly ahead—not so large and luxurious as the one at Vellanti, but infinitely welcome. But it was padlocked! The Contessa, however, was not to be discouraged. "We must break a window; you can crawl in to investigate, Megan?" Briskly, she led the way to the upper side and found a window fairly close to the ground. "It will be easy to get through; the only thing—what is underneath?" She flashed the torch briefly. "Tchk, what filthy windows! The Laurentis' watchman is *lazy*!" she remarked with deep disapproval. Handing the light to Megan, she drew off her glove—to remove the immense diamond from her ring finger. "Now we see," she remarked calmly—and cut a dashing oval in the pane. "Steady the light . . . ah, there we are." A section of the window disappeared with a tinkling crash. "Well, there is *something* there, at any rate," the Contessa observed optimistically.

Taking back the flashlight, she played it over the window, identified the fastening, and in a minute had thrust her hand through to open it. As it swung back, both women leaned forward to peer down. "Praises be!" said Megan.

There was a crosswalk directly beneath the window. Megan scrambled through the window, hung by her hands, and dropped about a foot . . . staggering but not (thank goodness) falling backward! "I think it's a bit far for you," she whispered upward to the blur of 'Tessa's white face. "Hand down the torch and let me prospect . . ."

There were two boats: a fancy launch beneath a canvas cover and a small rowboat in the near berth. The water doors had a snap lock and bars at the top and bottom. There were oars, but a cobwebbed boathook hung on the wall. Megan went back to the window and handed up the torch. "See if you can get down to the water, close to the doors . . ."

It took a full packet of matches before she could untie the painter, inch along to the water door, find a new spot to retie . . . and patiently squeeze the rope under the opened door. It was, infuriatingly, about two inches too short . . . but at last she'd managed it, pulled out and around, holding the door open with a rusty boathook until 'Tessa stepped in. "I relocked the window, just in case there's a watchman . . ." said 'Tessa.

Just as Megan was gently working the painter under the edge of the water door . . . searchlights rounded the point—a high-powered cruiser playing its beams back and forth along the shore . . .

"Lake Police: don't panic!" Megan told herself . . . But as she'd made it and was pulling the boat back into the berth . . . *Would they be able to see the Laurenti water doors swinging shut?* It couldn't be helped now—but if they found the cracked window, even though the Contessa had thought to refasten it, they might investigate.

Swiftly, untying the painter and inching along to retie in the usual spot, Megan said, "We daren't use the torch, but try to get into the next boat, under the tarpaulin . . ." She found the Contessa's hand and steadied her to step up to the crosswalk. "You still have the torch; don't leave anything behind . . ."

"I have it, but it does not matter," the Contessa said impersonally. "That is the Vellanti boat, Megan."

"The hell it is!" Megan stepped out boldly to the launch and found that the tarpaulin was the sort that battens down with metal fasteners. "Reach for the wall, 'Tessa, and move slowly this way." Rapidly she undid three of the fasteners and lifted the canvas slightly. "Come on . . . in you get—and they're still far enough away for us to use the torch for a minute . . . *quick!*" Silently, 'Tessa crawled down into the cockpit, made her way forward and flashed the torch about, while Megan reached out to fasten two of the catches easily and got a vicious scratch to the wrist as she worked her hand back in after the final catch . . . but at least the boat was normal to outward appearance.

The Contessa had moved down into the cabin, where there were two bunks piled with a gurry of life jackets, pillows, bathing towels, and crumbling rubber caps. The portholes were as filmed with dirt as the boathouse itself: good! Megan could begin to hear the engine of the Vellanti launch approaching. "Lie on a bunk; pretend you're stored for the winter," she hissed. Then she made a tasteful arrangement of towels and pillows over the inert body . . .

And faint but clear through the outer air, 'Renzo's

voice said, "Put in, Ugo—they might have made it . . ."

"Sì . . ." And by the cold impassivity of tone in the interchange, Megan *knew* that now they were hunting to kill, and for two men who had worked together in the Underground, nothing could be simpler than to throttle two women and leave their bodies to be found floating . . .

Nor would they be careless in any least detail. She could hear the launch tied up, sense the lights dimmed, and feel the silent motion about the boathouse . . . And she knew that they would find the broken window, and even though it was locked and seemed to be only a cracked pane due to winter freezing weather, they would check to be sure.

For a moment she held her breath, *listening* . . . certain she heard a muttered word, certain of a torch playing over the interior of the boathouse, and cowering on the floor of the cabin, certain at last of an infinitesimal "scroop" of metal on metal.

She heard the window catch sliding back . . .

Through the dirty cabin windows. 'Tessa's body might pass for a bundle of pillows and sails, but there was no cover for Megan—except . . . She crawled forward and inched open a door with her heart in her mouth . . . but miraculously, the door made no sound.

It was nearly as soundless as the tiny thud of rubber-soled shoes dropping . . . padding toward her.

Megan sat on the toilet.

It smelled.

She held the door in gloved fingers, and even as a flashlight searched the cabin through the portholes, sending a sliver of light into the crack of Megan's

171

door, she thought—as disapprovingly as the Contessa: "the Laurentis are lousy housekeepers . . ."

Would 'Renzo and Ugo unfasten the cockpit cover? Apparently they were debating—but there was suddenly another snort of approaching engines . . . from Como, judging by the sound. Instantly, light footsteps ran along the crosswalk in retreat, up and out the window. Then the catch was thrown shut heedless of noise . . . But even as Megan felt faint with reprieve, she recognized the lasting effects of Commando, Underground training.

"*Olà*, what occurs? Prince di Frecchia, there is something wrong?"

Megan inched open her door, as she heard the breath of a whisper, "*That* is the Lake police . . ."

"Don't change position—they may return for an official search . . ."

"Captain Conti, thank God you are here!" 'Renzo's voice was no longer dispassionate but distracted with tragedy. "We fear the worst! Mama has apparently gone for a moonlight boat ride with her American protégée—without a word to *anyone* . . . and now we find the boat overturned and floating! For an hour we are searching the shore, in hopes they may have survived and found shelter somewhere . . ."

"But this is madness, Prince di Frecchia!" The police captain's voice was austere with disapproval. "*For an hour? Why* did you not notify us *at once?* You have the ship telephone . . . Pietro." There were sounds of muffled directions, a distant chattering code signal, and 'Renzo's broken sobs. "Calm yourself, Prince di Frecchia! Where does this occur, is it known when they departed?"

"The boat is in the Mordino Cove," replied Ugo's voice, "and it is not precise, but they have left after twelve thirty, for then I spoke to la Contessa myself."

"Still—Mordino? What do you *here?* If they reach shore, they turn for Vellanti . . ."

"Two women after such a shock—perhaps they become confused in the darkness," said Ugo.

"Two women in the darkness after such an experience could never have come so far," the captain's voice was faintly impatient. Again searchlights played over the boathouse. "See for yourselves: doors secured, no sign of life—if they were here, would they not call out to us? No, they will be completely in the other direction. Please to come with us, Prince di Frecchia, adding your lights to ours until the Bellagio police can meet us."

At long last, the two boats cast off and turned back to Vellanti, *but* . . . "*Still* don't move!" Megan whispered, inching open her door once more and listening as if her life depended upon it—which, very possibly, it did.

Because *she* might not be able to handle the Vellanti power launch alone, but Prince Lorenzo di Frecchia was a man . . . and one dedicated to his own survival, which would probably lend him extra strength . . . and in the darkness, what was to prevent Ugo's dropping off the launch, to return silently for a definitive check of the Laurenti boathouse? Might he not be waiting patiently, quietly, outside—for the deep breath of relief, the long stretch and yawn from the two women they were hunting?

There was no sound, no light, but Megan was now trying to outguess a killer of the Underground. It might prove wasted tension, but there was no longer any slightest doubt in her mind that this was the point of no return.

Tonight was the night—*because they'd made a run for it*, she realized sickly. Neither she nor the Contessa could be allowed, now, to reach *anyone*—however stupid. Because it wasn't war time, though, at least 'Renzo and Ugo couldn't kill *everyone* who happened to show up at the wrong moment, even if they didn't know what was going on . . .

"What was Ugo's method of killing?" she thought analytically. Hands, perhaps—or a knife—but probably not a gun, because of modern ballistics being able to identify . . .

"Where," asked the Contessa very, very softly, "was Cesare?"

CHAPTER ELEVEN

That was a good question . . .

There'd been no sound of Cesare. Had he stayed out of sight in the launch, ready to reinforce his brother—or was it he rather than Ugo who had slipped ashore, completely unsuspected by Captain Conti and his men?

Megan thought not. If anyone had been left behind, it would be Ugo—who knew all the silent ways of death. Still what could he do, aside from holding them trapped until 'Renzo could shake off the police? It was imperative, now, for the Contessa's demise to be an unimpeachable accident. Nor could it occur here, when the Lake Police had just examined the place, for then there were bound to be very awkward questions . . . In fact, there would be very awkward questions if Ugo were not in evidence beside his master right this minute.

Which left only Cesare unaccounted for. "One if by land, and two if by sea," said Megan's mind . . . and of course that would be *it*. Prince di Frecchia and Ugo would have to accept the police and aid the search with enthusiasm, leaving no stone unturned and playing all the way through to the final scene of 'Renzo's tottering figure being led back to Casa Grande, amid loud weeping and wailings . . . Dr.

Silvio would be required for sedation; Vellanti would go into mourning . . .

Prince Cesare would be absent, however, and Ugo would be sent, ostensibly to break the tragic news. And then—they would retrace every inch—because it was not entirely certain that the women were here, after all. Captain Conti's arrival had siphoned off the definitive search—blessed Captain Conti!

Within the smelly toilet, Megan found a match and inspected her watch: it was nearly four A.M.—about an hour before there would be sufficient light for her to try for help. It might be enough . . .

Reinforced by the Bellagio police boat, Captain Conti would keep 'Renzo and Ugo occupied in a thorough search, with no way to let Cesare know they were treed, stymied, up the creek and *hors de combat.*

Why not? Because Cesare was patrolling the main roads in a car? Perhaps—but even if he were afoot in the woods, he'd have to keep out of sight, or Captain Conti would immediately immobilize him by adding him to the search—and if he had to be unseen, there could be no way for Ugo to impart the latest development to him. Cesare'd know only that the police were aware that la Contessa was missing . . .

Furthermore, Megan had a hunch Cesare would have been put ashore in the Mordino cove, to go afoot through the woods and underbrush *toward* Vellanti, while 'Renzo and Ugo in the launch explored toward Como . . . just in case. So Cesare was now walking farther and farther away from the Laurenti boathouse, with no way for the others to redirect him. Good!

Even better, if Cesare were out on the road in a

car . . . he'd be totally unreachable until Ugo could slip away in another car to hunt for him . . .

Megan sat on the cabin floor. "I think you can dare to change position now, if you're cramped," she whispered, "but I'm afraid we're trapped till dawn. As soon as I can see without a flashlight, I'll try for a phone. There might be one in the main house, or perhaps the watchman . . . Could you sleep? Are you warm enough?"

"I'm *suffocating!*" the Contessa whispered energetically. "*Never* did I realize the Laurentis were such filthy pigs—one of these pillows smells like the lavabo in a bordello!"

She slithered thankfully onto the deck while Megan asked, "How would *you* know about bordellos?"

"My husband told me," 'Tessa whispered blandly, her hand fumbling for Megan's.

"Oh, *don't!* I'll get the giggles!" Megan sat silently holding the Contessa's hand for a long moment, aware of the dreadful stuffiness of the cabin, but ruthlessly refusing to acknowledge her weariness—for she mustn't fall asleep and miss the moment to get assistance . . .

"Are we safe for a while, do you think?"

"Yes, thanks to Captain Conti." Softly, Megan outlined her reasoning. "Try to rest, 'Tessa."

"How can I? Why Lorenzo, Megan?"

"Because he's mortgaged Frecchia to the hilt and stands to lose it by foreclosure in a few weeks."

"Oh, NO!"

"Shhh, I'm sorry but—yes. I only learned this morning. I'd have learned anyway, they never stopped my mail, but I burned the letter so they don't know I know."

"I knew there was something in these past years—I never dreamed it was so bad. Yesterday—the pictures were gone: the Caravaggio, all the Renoirs, the Ghirlandaio . . . I did not ask," she muttered. *"Perhaps* Cesare is restoring or repairing frames, but I know it is not so. They have been sold, Megan." She gripped Megan's hand, agonized. "And now—who will have the palazzo?"

"An oily pig from Arkansas, according to Uncle Joe —and the business is probably bankrupt, too."

"That I had suspected—but *not Frecchia.* Megan, we have to get out of here. I must do something. *Not Frecchia!"* The Contessa struggled to sit up on the bunk, while Megan murmured "Shhhhh."

"In Frecchia my children were born, I was happy, I loved it next to Vellanti," the Contessa whispered. She was speaking Italian unconsciously, yet Megan understood because she was a woman, too. "Lucius was my dear companion, but Uberto was my *love."*

"So long we lived there . . . and my gardens! There were herbs and roses, and mountain plants that Uberto brought me—a pleached walk of plane trees finer than at Arconati, and espaliered fruit trees about the walls . . . seats everywhere from which to look at *mi Lago di Como* while eating a fresh apricot.

"When Uberto died, Cesare and I returned to Vellanti. 'Renzo decided to live in New York for the business, and later, when I married Lucius, we were mostly in America. I did not know what was happening. It seemed sensible to rent the palazzo for a few months, it gave employment to our staff. Then it became a constant affair. On my few visits to Vellanti, always there were tenants when I wished to stop at Frecchia, only for a moment . . .

"And one tenant replaces the herbs with cannas . . . and another had the rose sneezes, so the bushes are removed. The mountain plants have grown wild because no one cares. I no longer asked to see Frecchia."

The Contessa was frankly sobbing softly, her head bent against Megan's shoulder. "Cesare visits occasionally when 'Renzo is away and tenants have left—so kind, *mi Cesare!* He never forgets to write me of new babies or the death of an old friend, but now—I think he does not know of this either."

Privately, Megan wondered. She had a sneaking hunch Prince Cesare was perfectly capable of figuring out his brother's difficulties, and would say nothing to his mama until he had the money for Szirbino!

"Frecchia is all I have left of Uberto," the Contessa said with sudden clarity, "and even if I am never let to see it myself again, *I will not let it go!*

"That is why." The Contessa fumbled for a handkerchief, blew her nose vigorously, and sat up on the bunk. "I cannot explain, I do not even know why— but for some reason Lorenzo does not want *me* to be connected with Frecchia. Perhaps—you do not know our family, Megan—nor wish to, I'm sure, poor child! But always Lorenzo . . . He is not *tall*," she finished, simply.

"I see. Well, so far we've been lucky, and I think God is still with us," Megan said calmly, "so I shall now unfasten the tarpaulin and take a peek."

Quietly, she made her way into the cockpit and chose a fastener on the side away from the broken window, but it was a painful task: the Laurentis might be filthy pigs, but they'd spend money for a canvas built to fit—damn them!

Eventually she'd got one of the pins open and she could reach to the next and the next and twitch the cover up to assess . . . There was a definite lightness beyond the dirty windows and no sound but lapping water. Megan's watch said a quarter to five; by the time she'd reached the main house, surely some-one would be awake?

This was it. Megan went back to whisper, "I'm going now; I'll fasten you in—if anyone comes, duck into the head and lock the door after you . . . you'd better not dare smoke a cigarette, or they'll smell it at once!"

"*Bonne chance, ma fille.*" The Contessa's dark eyes flashed faintly in the dimness of the cabin, and she held out her arms. As Megan bent forward for a hug and kiss, 'Tessa said, "God be with you, *cara.*"

"He is," Megan chuckled. "There's a ladder to reach the window!" She made her way aft, slipped out to the crosswalk and battened down the tarpaulin once more. Then she went along the crosswalk to the window and could hear no sound. She set the ladder against the wall and got herself up and out to the open air—but she still had the boathook. Very care-fully she leaned down, gently connected the hook with the ladder and once more laid the thing on its side— approximately where it had been originally.

Perhaps Ugo would not notice such a small altera-tion? But that he would know—if he returned—that there had been a ladder lying against the wall under the broken window, Megan had no doubt! She closed the catch of the window and crawled to the edge of the boathouse . . . and she still had the damned boat-hook . . .

She would have to take it along and thrust it some-where among the shrubbery . . . Ahead of her was an unmistakable path, and as paths generally go some-where, Megan stood up and plunged into it. The gradient was far steeper than the one at Vellanti, but she collected her strength and went steadily ahead until she emerged on a flight of steps leading to a terrace beside the Laurenti villa. There were the inevitable marble pillars; Megan leaned against the lowest one and panted for breath, simultaneously surveying the scene.

The view was not so far-reaching as at Vellanti, but she could see that there was no motion near the boathouse. Good! She could see as far as Cernobbia, where the milk and newspaper delivery men were apparently putting forth. Good, again—the more small boats there were on the lake, the more inconvenient explanations would have to be made!

Megan's heart lifted—she needed only a telephone; she would ruthlessly awaken Dr. Innisperg's Embassy friend in Rome . . . She swung around to contemplate a pair of unmistakable walking boots whose wearer (by the stance) was equally contemplating *her*. The Laurenti watchman! Megan raised her head eagerly, and faced Prince Cesare di Frecchia.

For a moment she simply stared at him . . . but if it was over, it was over. "Well, well—and where were *you* when the lights went out?"

"What have you done with my mother?"

"Made her into cutlets for the deep freeze, and now if you'll excuse me, I have to see a Graham cracker about a Bell?" Megan darted sideways. Where in hell was the Laurenti watchman? Obviously not where he was needed . . . and in three steps Cesare di Frecchia had her shoulders, whirling her to face him.

"Mama is in the boathouse?"

"Yes," Megan positioned the boathook as best she could and looked at Cesare defiantly, "but before you get to her, you'll have to kill me—and I warn you, I've written the *whole story* to Uncle Joe and

181

Dr. Innisperg, so you won't get away with anything."

"What are you talking about?" he said violently, his fingers plucking the boathook from her hand and tossing it aside. "*Stupida!* All I want is to make her safe. Why do you not *tell* me Mama is frightened, instead of this nonsense in the night?"

"I didn't know which of you it was," Megan said— and writhed, screaming involuntarily as his fingers bit down into her shoulders.

"You . . . you *nothing!*" Cesare choked—and shook her like a rag doll. "How dare you think *I* will harm Mama? And you . . . you drag her through woods and night air; she is not young, and her chest not strong. . . . If she catches a cold, if your *stupidity* puts her in the hospital," Cesare's fingers literally picked her up and shook her like a puppy, "I'll never forgive you for the rest of my life, *no matter how much I love you—d'you hear?*" With a final shake, he discarded her, half throwing her into the shrubbery and striding forward, down the path. It was a moment before Megan recovered herself.

"Oh, *do* you?" she gasped involuntarily, stumbling after him, "because I do, too . . . love you, I mean . . ." Cesare stopped and whirled around. "She's quite safe, *truly* . . ." Megan said pleadingly, "Please . . ."

"*Carissima* . . ."

For a moment, Megan rested against him, clung to his lips, knowing he was good and he was *hers*. "We must get 'Tessa," she murmured vaguely. "I would much rather kiss you, but I expect we can do that later?"

"*Si, mi dilètta*," he agreed, straight-faced. "Later— and forever, or as long as you like." Megan could feel herself reddening, but Cesare only threw back his head and laughed deeply, catching Megan against him in a strong arm. For an instant he turned, setting his fingers to his lips and whistling sharply three times. "Now we will rescue Mama."

"What was that whistling?"

"It summons the men of Vellanti who came with me to find their Contessa," he said quietly. "You are not the only one to whom Mama is important . . . Shall we go?"

Silently, Megan fitted her steps to Cesare's long stride as best she could. "How did you know?"

"Anna Maria. She kept watch, and when she saw the launch drawn out to follow you, she came to tell me." They were nearly to the boathouse now, and Megan could hear rapid footsteps and voices above and behind them . . . She could feel herself trembling uncontrollably. Oh, it was not *possible* to think she might have led 'Tessa into a trap, a plot in which all Vellanti would back its manager against its owner . . . and she no longer had even the rusty boathook . . .

Megan caught her breath in a sob of fright. Oh, she had been stupid—*stupid* . . . Was she always to be thrown off balance merely by a kiss, a man to sweet-talk her? First Bob . . . now this Cesare . . . She must forget the strong arm about her, forget the warm lips, the words of love—she'd promised to protect the Contessa, and at the first hint of romance, she'd forgotten everything. Dimly, she could hear engines churning through the water . . . or did she? If only it were Captain Conti, there might still be a chance to save 'Tessa . . . poor darling, sitting in that horrid cabin, probably terrified by the noise outside . . .

"*Carissima*, I go too fast for you—forgive me," Cesare said, as Megan stumbled against him. "Ah, you are so tired, my sweet love! If only you had told me . . ." He sighed with frustration, but he was still smiling and looking down at her half-incredulous. "To try to do so much alone," he muttered. "You sweet clever little devil!" Once more Megan was caught against him, feeling the body, the lips, the murmur that spells home for any woman . . .

"*There they are!*" shouted Lorenzo's voice . . . falsetto, shaking with accusation. "It is as I told you, Captain Conti! This woman . . . and my brother— she has hypnotized him, I assure you!" Prince di Frecchia was scrambling awkwardly from the Vellanti launch, striding forward to point a commanding finger at Megan and Cesare . . . with Captain Conti and his men deploying rapidly into a ring about them.

Where was Ugo?

"Prince Cesare, I regret . . . a few questions, and of *la Signorina* also?"

"Come, come, Conti—questions can be asked at the Police Bureau . . . the situation is obvious; you saw for yourself . . ."

"If you please, Prince di Frecchia, there are certain formalities to be complied with . . ."

Cesare's deep voice mingled with the trampling of feet lining up behind him, 'Renzo's falsetto squeak and Captain Conti's harassed attempt to restore order . . .

Megan leaned against Cesare's arm and felt her eyes closing from weariness. There were so many people, so many voices; it was Grand Central Station and *everyone* was here, rushing for the commuter trains to Scarsdale and Larchmont and Westport . . . Everyone, everyone . . .

Except the Contessa—*and Ugo* . . .

Megan opened her eyes and screamed, *"Shut up, you fools!"* Frantically, she pulled free of Cesare and bolted for the broken window . . . *to find it swinging free.* So Ugo was already inside the boathouse . . . and there were hands pulling her back inexorably. "Miss Royce, please control yourself!"

"La Contessa . . . Captain Conti, *please* release her . . . save her . . ."

"But you are not pretending she is still *alive?"*

"Of course she's alive," Megan sobbed wildly, "but not for lack of trying to kill her—eh Prince di Frecchia?"

"I do not understand you, Signorina. You *confess* that you and your lover, Prince Cesare, have attempted . . ."

". . . To save la Contessa from murder at the hands of her son Lorenzo, Prince di Frecchia, and his henchman Ugo . . . and Prince Cesare is not my lover, I never saw him before in my life," Megan cried frantically. *"Please* don't stand here *talking!* Open the boathouse before Ugo reaches her, please, please . . ."

"You see? It is as I told you, Captain Conti: the girl is a neurotic, of the hysterical type. We knew nothing of her; Mama brings her from Paris on a whim— and now she has the audacity even to accuse me, Prince di Frecchia!" 'Renzo shouted dramatically, dashing about as the police aides tried to pass him . . . But already Cesare had violently thrown off restraining hands and the men from Vellanti were prying off the padlock and throwing open the doors . . .

"By all means use your title," Megan said wearily. "It's all you have left, isn't it, Prince di Frecchia? *Isn't it?"*

"This girl *raves*—pay no attention . . . Poor thing! she has no idea what she says . . . be gentle with her, I beg of you . . ."

"The hell I don't know what I'm saying," Megan stated. "I'm saying Prince di Frecchia is bankrupt—and unless Ugo has managed to kill the Contessa so that Prince di Frecchia will inherit a third of her fortune, while you've been dilly-dallying out here, he will be a prince without a seat to sit in . . . because Frecchia will be foreclosed by an American oil baron."

"Oh, what *madness* is this!" 'Renzo groaned. "Captain Conti, I hired this girl in New York, knowing nothing of her but that she had been ill . . . Oh, it is my fault that I do not check, to learn it is a mental illness . . ."

"Oh, piffle," Megan said rudely, "I had an appendectomy, that is all—and it was my doctor who found out you were bankrupt and about to lose Frecchia . . ." Before she could continue, there was a triumphant shout and, a minor procession came from the boathouse—the men of Vellanti came swaggering happily behind the tall figure of Cesare, who was carrying the Contessa in his arms.

Unconsciously, the hands fell away from Megan's arms, and she ran forward. "'Tessa, you are safe?"

"Entirely, my dear. Put me down now, Cesare. Ah, Captain Conti, how pleased to see you . . . but where is Lorenzo? Surely I heard his voice?" The Contessa was white-faced, but she was still completely, aristocratically in control—and Lorenzo was gone.

In a split second, he was entirely, most horribly gone . . . when the Vellanti launch, into which he had dashed under cover of the jubilation over the Contessa's appearance, rammed a stanchion and exploded into a hideous sheet of flame. While Captain Conti and his men raced for the police boats, Megan threw her arms about 'Tessa. "Don't look . . ." she cried.

"No, but don't grieve, my dear. What is that saying? 'Better death than dishonor . . .'" The Contessa drew a *long*, sobbing breath and steadied her shoulders. "Cesare? I should like to go home. Is it possible?"

Amazingly, it was not too difficult for Megan to put on a dinner dress, after a long sleep and a warm bath . . . Nor was it impossible to put the last twenty-four hours out of her mind . . . Only when Megan was picking up her lipstick did her hand begin to shake. She stared at herself in the mirror and saw a small-boned, anomalous female, with hair-colored hair and eye-colored eyes . . . She saw *nothing* to recommend her to a prince.

She knew she must forget Cesare—he had only used a tactic to save the situation; at that moment he'd have tried *anything*, and he had been clever enough to know that "romance" would work with silly Megan. Well, 'Tessa was safe, and Megan could pack and leave, as soon as she'd cleaned up around the edges. There would be a pretense-normal dinner this evening, polite protests from the Contessa, and firm explanations from Megan . . . "The Zhondeks; you remember I told you of them? I must meet them. It is all arranged." It would be bad enough for the Contessa to be forced to endure this final evening—to look at the girl who'd caused the death of her son . . .

No longer was Ugo at the great grilled doors of the castle . . . There was no more Lorenzo, posturing before the mantel in the small salon and bustling forward to receive Megan as head of the house, while Cesare stood politely aside . . .

Megan set her teeth, threw up her chin, and went steadily into the room—to stop dead, as Cardinal di Frecchia turned in a swirl of red robes to face her. Beside him, 'Tessa smiled from the depths of her easy chair . . . behind him, Cesare's dark eyes looked at Megan intently . . . "Come in, my child." Numbly, Megan went forward, was enfolded in the kindly arms.

"I—am happy to see you again, Your Eminence . . ."

"And I to see you . . . it has been a very dreadful day, for you as well as the rest of us, but now it is over. In the midst of life we are in death—but I like to think that even when there is death, there is life," he said softly, smiling down at her. "We are inclined to formality in Italy, Megan; you know that? So I have come, as Head of the Family, to ask that you accept the hand of my nephew Cesare in marriage."

There was a seemingly endless pause, while Megan looked from one face to another, meeting the Contessa's great dark eyes, which were shadowed with pain. "You could never forget . . . you can't want *me*," she whispered, frantically. "It was only a—joke, to get me to tell you where your mother was," she said to Cesare.

"I do not joke in these matters," Cesare said evenly. "Do you?"

"No, of course not! But how can you bear to look at me?" She turned to the Contessa. "You can't really want me."

"It has not gone as I anticipated," the Contessa said, "but otherwise . . ." She smiled wickedly. "Why *else* d'you think I bring you to Vellanti, Megan darling? Cesare, what are you about? Convince her, please . . ."

Dell Bestsellers

At last the sequel to *Beulah Land*
is now in paperback!

LOOK AWAY, BEULAH LAND

by **Lonnie Coleman**

For the plantation of Beulah Land and its masters, the Civil
War ended in humiliation and destruction. Here are the
characters you loved in the original story: Sarah Kendrick,
the iron inspiration behind the struggle to rebuild the
plantation; Benjamin Davis, determined to be his own
man and strong enough to let no one stop him; Daniel Todd,
a Union deserter; and Nancy, the freed slave whose
toughness and gaiety lead her to a Savannah brothel.

Bound together by the affections of generations, Beulah
Land's men and women set about creating a new way of
life in *Look Away, Beulah Land*—a blend of past and
future, perhaps stronger than the one they once knew.

A Dell Book $2.50

At your local bookstore or use this handy coupon for ordering:

The Far Side of Destiny

by Dore Mullen

His arms wrapped her in a breathless embrace, his èyes burned into her soul and Daria knew he was her fate. In one passion-swept moment her past vanished. Now, there was only this desperate journey across a revolution-ravaged tundra. And there was only Nicholas, this handsome worldly stranger they called the Man of Ice. By train across Siberia, fleeing Cossack regiments and Bolshevik partisans, Daria discovered a world of luxury and intrigue—a world in which the man she loved became an elegant stranger.

A Dell Book $2.25

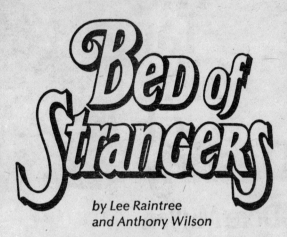